FINDING THE TROLL'S HEART

TROLLKIN LOVERS

BOOK SIX

LYONNE RILEY

INTRODUCTION

Six months ago, Simka's sister was stolen by wild orcs. When the neutral city of Morgenzan refuses to help, Simka takes it upon herself to go on a rescue mission—but she can't find the orc camp alone.

Corporal Jar'kel, a grouchy old troll with a broken tusk, has been sent to the frigid Blue Crags to help defend a valuable mine against the wild orcs. When he catches Simka vandalizing the mine, he makes her a deal: if she helps him find the wild orcs, he'll help save her sister, and he can at last return home.

While Jar'kel and Simka work together to locate the orc camp, Jar'kel denies his growing attraction to the younger human woman. But to succeed in their mission, they must pretend to be a mated pair. Can they keep up the ruse when it feels much too real?

CONTENT WARNINGS

- Age gap
- Virgin FMC

- Virginity loss
- Painful sex
- Bonded mates
- Voyeurism
- Public sexual acts
- Killing of animals for meat and pelts (off-page)
- Violence
- Arson
- Torture (off-page)
- Gore (dismembered head)
- Life-threatening pregnancy
- Breeding
- Pregnancy
- Lactation play
- Birth

Chapter 1

Simka

My sister was not the first woman to be taken from our village, but not to sound like an asshole, she was the one who meant the most to me.

When the wild orcs came six months ago, streaming down the mountain like an avalanche, Vavi shoved me into the cellar. "I'll distract them," she said hurriedly. "Whatever happens, Simka, don't make a sound."

So I stayed silent as I could as she locked the door firmly behind her. I listened, hand clamped over my mouth, as the orcs thundered into the house, snatched her, and dragged her away.

Vavi didn't fight, or even protest. The orcs growled words in a language I couldn't understand, and then left, slamming the door closed behind them.

How my sister was so brave, I'll never know.

I sat there shivering, wondering if Dad would survive. He was among the villagers defending the town, and the wild orcs outnumbered us—and they were bigger, stronger, and meaner.

For some reason, though, the orcs left Dad and the others alive. The invaders only seemed interested in two things: our food supplies, and the people they stole. Along with another young woman and a young man, Vavi was gone.

It was Dad who unlocked the cellar door, gun still in his hand, begging to know what had become of my sister. I had to tell him the awful truth that she gave her life for mine. We had collapsed to the floor together in tears, and I've had to live with it ever since. I was willing to be silent while she was taken away.

Now it's my only job to find her and get her back. That's why I'm once again trying to climb this massive sheet of ice. But my pack is too heavy, and I'm only twenty feet up when I have to navigate my way back down or my arms will give out.

I've been trying to trace the wild orcs' tracks back to their camp for months. After the attack, they retreated into the snow-covered Blue Crags, the immense mountains that stand sentinel over our village. The very same night the orcs ran off with Vavi, I pulled on my boots, mittens, and cloak through my tears, and followed their prints. But the path was weaving, and quickly got lost in the rocky cliffs. That same night, their trail was buried under a fresh layer of snow, and I lost them.

Still, I had a heading, and that gave me hope that if I could climb deeper into the mountains, I'd eventually find it. But the Crags are immense and treacherous, and only a fool would put themselves in danger by venturing too far into them. I've already gone farther afield than I should searching for any sign of the camp, and Dad would certainly not approve if he knew. He's even forbidden me from going after Vavi, because he knows too well that I'll risk my life to find her, and he can't bear the idea of losing another daughter.

Not that I've ever really listened to him.

But I keep meeting the same roadblock: the sharp, icy rock faces that lead even higher into the mountains. When I finally have my feet back under me again and I'm standing on the firm ground, I curse and throw my picks into the snow.

No one else in the village thinks it's worthwhile to search for our missing people. Most of my neighbors believe they're dead already—or perhaps something even worse. Though we weren't the only village attacked by the wild orcs, when we sent a letter to the city of Morgenzan for help... they ignored us.

The city guard of the biggest neutral city in the world, the very people supposed to help and protect us, did nothing.

The snow turns the color of fire as another fruitless day comes to an end. I head down the icy slopes toward home, my shoulders sagging. The hills spread out around me, covered in endless evergreen trees, their branches frosted with snow.

Tomorrow will be different. It has to be. I'll pack less, just the bare essentials. Or I'll practice my pull-ups until I'm strong enough. Or I'll keep walking south until I find another way up.

I will find her.

On my way home, I check my traps. Though I'm not one of our village's primary hunters, I've been training in hope they'll take me on a hunt someday. I bring in animals from time to time as proof I can do this. Dad says we don't need any more wolf or badger pelts, and they're too much work to clean and cure, but I'm going to keep bringing them home until I land something better.

When I locate my trap, though, it's empty. Damn it. Sometimes it all feels hopeless, like I'm chasing after a ghost.

It's late when I finally return to the little house I share with Dad. My mule, Fio, greets me over the railing of his pen. He's sturdy and strong, with copious, thick fur covering every inch of his body. His sire was one of the stout, hairy ponies that call the mountains home, and his dam was an ass that a merchant had brought with him from out of town. This bizarre combination created a surprisingly perfect steed for the snowy slopes. I pet his nose and scratch behind his ears, just the way he likes, before going inside.

"You're back." Dad rises from the table where he's been cleaning his gun. It's his most valuable possession, as difficult as it is to get firearms up here in the Blue Crags. "What have you been doing all day?" he asks, the same way he does every day, with an arch in his brow. I wonder if he knows I've been out looking for Vavi.

I shake my head and shrug. "Followed some tracks, but found nothing. Traps are empty."

He falls back into his chair. "Well, at least you didn't bring home another rabbit. We're full up on mittens." Thoughtfully, he taps a finger on the table. "I heard today that the Grand Chieftain sent even more soldiers. Supposedly, they're going to help the beef up the city guard, and keep the wild orcs away from the mine."

I can't help a snarl. Those infernal trollkin built a mining operation not far from Morgenzan, tearing open one of our beautiful mountains to pillage it for resources. They shouldn't have been allowed to do it in the first place, not on neutral territory— but they did anyway, and now they rely on the city guard to protect it.

"Neutral" my ass. The Blue Crags might be contested territory in wartime, but we humans have always lived here. *They* are the invaders. The trollkin don't belong here, and yet the city guard care more about protecting the Grand Chieftain's mine than about human lives.

Then it occurs to me: more soldiers arriving, even if they're all trollkin, also means more bodies. Maybe now that they're properly armed and staffed, the city guard might be willing to send out search parties. Wherever my sister is, the wild orcs are there, too. It would benefit all of us.

It's a hike from our village to the fortress of Morgenzan, but perhaps if I can supply information about the direction the orcs fled, we'd have a shot at finding them. Maybe this is my chance to get real help.

When I go into our bedroom, Vavi's bed is, as always, empty. Before she was kidnapped, I thought certainly she'd be getting married soon, and then I'd get to have our room to myself. She would pick one of the many boys who had drooled over her through our adolescence, say her vows under the holly, and move out. She's always been the beautiful one, the one that they talked in hushed voices about marrying.

But now she'll never have the chance, not unless I can get her back. I refuse to believe she's dead. My sister is a survivor, like me.

For the first time in months, I go to bed feeling comforted that I have a plan.

JAR'KEL

The truth is trolls are simply not meant for cold places.

We were designed for the jungle, to run around in nothing but our loincloths and jewels, to hunt what we need, to bathe in warm rivers and streams. I've even accepted the vast and inhospitable desert, where I'm typically stationed, because my body can tolerate the heat much better than it can the cold.

Trolls are certainly not meant to be trudging through snow up to our waists. I'm dressed in a new military coat I was issued on the train, but still every last inch of me is frigid and numb, and there's an itchy sensation spreading from my toes and fingers into my feet and hands. There's a long way to go to Morgenzan—it's much too soon to turn into an icicle.

"A little chilly there, corporal?" asks one of the orcs on my team. He's a big, heavy-set fellow who was sent here from some other part of the world. His name isn't important to me, as the moment this mission is finished, I intend to return to my original post in the desert of the Hazrain. There's a lot to do now that we've lost the captain of the city guard and the lieutenant both. It's been difficult to replace them.

A very odd and surprising thing, the captain and the lieutenant finding each other. I'd never before seen, or even heard of, an orc and a human engaging in that sort of relationship. One of the world's great mysteries, I suppose.

They seemed happy, despite the fact they'll never be accepted by either human or trollkin kind. No, they've chosen to simply live their lives together, even have whelps together, in a neutral city. When I came across my former lieutenant in the market one day, his daughter sitting on his shoulders, he looked happier than I've ever seen him.

Not that I'll ever know what that's like. I gave up on having a life like that for myself a long time ago. I'm too old now, and much too foul-tempered.

"If you're not cold right now," I snap back at the irritating orc next to me, "you're lying."

He chuckles. "I guess orcs are made of sturdier stuff than trolls." I want to punch the smug look right off his face. Not only is the cold slowly eating away at my extremities, but it's making me bitter and grouchy, even more than usual.

But this discomfort is temporary. With so many of us swarming to the frigid north to rectify this pesky wild orc problem, I'm sure we'll be able to defeat them in time for dinner. A few brutes won't get between the Grand Chieftain and his gold—and we're just his pawns.

That night by the fire, I check to make sure my toes are still attached, then hang my boots up to dry. Back home I don't even wear shoes, because what's the point? The sand doesn't bother my tough feet, but trying to walk in the snow without boots would leave me with four frozen-off toes.

"How'd you lose the tusk?" the annoying orc asks, not that I've given him any indication I still want to talk. He flops down by the fire beside me, taking a swig from a flask.

I push my feet closer to the fire, not acknowledging him. But he's unperturbed. "Bad fight?" he pushes. "A trolless, maybe?"

"No," I say through gritted teeth. "As if I'd take a blow like that for some pussy."

When I was young, my answer might have been different. There was a trolless, once, with a shock of purple hair wound into braids and a big, toothy smile. Her cunt had been so perfect around my cock. She would moan and scream as I took her as mine.

But like all things, that passion faded. After a few years we grew bored of each other, and I realized, perhaps too late, that we shared very little except pleasures of the body. When even the fucking became tedious, she decided she wanted someone younger —a troll with a little more pep in his step. So we said an unpleasant goodbye, and that was the last time I saw a pair of breasts.

"Then what?" the orc asks, peering at me curiously. "How'd you get a whole tusk snapped off?"

I might as well tell him, or he won't leave me alone. "Without that tusk, I wouldn't have a face left."

The orc's eyes widen. "It saved your life?"

"'Saved' is a relative term," I say, snatching away his flask and taking a big swig for myself. I barely made it out of the bandit raid alive, and all the goods we'd tasked with protecting were taken.

I'm still not sure why I stayed in the desert after that. Perhaps I was just too tired to leave again. As I began learning the human language, Freysian—which is somewhat of a necessity in a neutral city—I applied to work in the city guard.

Everyone has to make a living.

"At least you survived," the orc says, reclining in the snow, "so you could go on to fuck another day."

I bark a laugh. Idiot whelp. "If you think an orcess or a trolless wants anything to do with a troll who's only got one tusk, you're a moron." I hand the flask back to him, and he takes it with a grunt. "Now fuck off. I'm going to bed."

I leave before he can say anything else. We have a long day ahead tomorrow, and it'll probably take all the grit I have left.

I'm too old for this shit.

CHAPTER 2

SIMKA

Early the next morning, I saddle up Fio and pack some supplies that'll last me until I get back. I lie to Dad, telling him I'm going out to hunt again, and Fio and I begin the long haul to Morgenzan.

We walk all day, the snow reflecting the sunshine until it's nearly blinding. Around late afternoon, I spy the high stone walls that surround the city, almost indistinguishable from the mountain.

When we've made our way down the slope to the front gates, I hop off Fio and lead him by the reins. Behind the impenetrable wall, people traverse winding pathways carved into the mountainside, heading home at the end of a long day. I don't have any goods with me to be taxed, so the guards let me through without much fuss.

Morgenzan never ceases to amaze me. The whole mountain has been shaped to fit the city. Homes are built into the side, their low doorways dotting the road that crawls up from the base of the mountain to the top, where the city council resides. That's where I'll have to go to get the help I need.

Fio has no problem with heights, thankfully, so he plods along behind me without objection as we make our way up the many switchbacks leading to the top of the mountain. The pathways are surprisingly wide, allowing carts through with ease.

I like to think I'm fit and well-traveled, but even I'm gasping for air by the time we reach our destination. I'm already exhausted from my day of riding, and when I look around, there's nowhere to tie him. Damn it.

The only one nearby is a member of the city guard: a rather ugly blue trollkin with grooves at the corners of his eyes and mouth, and one broken-off tusk. What remains is cracked, the blunt end splintered. This guy's clearly seen some things in his life. He has dark blue hair that's short on top and thick at his sideburns, with a bit of his hairline pulling back.

I don't see trollkin often, not unless I'm visiting the city, and their big tusks and orange-red eyes always take me by surprise.

"Can you hold him for me?" I ask. At least as a soldier in a neutral city, he'll know how to speak Freysian. It's the bare minimum requirement.

He scowls, which deepens his wrinkles further. "I'm not a damn stablehand," he gripes, shoving Fio toward me. He grumbles something in Trollkin I can't understand, probably an insult.

I don't blame him. Maybe our peoples have settled on a reluctant truce, but that doesn't mean we have anything in common. It certainly doesn't mean we have to get along. At least, as persnickety as Fio is, he'd never let himself be stolen.

I shove the reins back into the troll's hands. "Come on, I just need a few minutes." His glare grows even more deadly. "It's urgent."

Without waiting for him to protest, I turn and duck into city council in the hope that somebody will help me.

"We've got our own wild orc problem," the guy behind the desk says in his most bored tone. "Your sister's gone, kid. She's dead."

I'm not a kid. Everyone thinks I am, because I'm short and my face is rounder than it should be for a woman my age, and I like to keep my hair cropped close so I don't have to manage it. I huff at him and ask to speak to his boss, but he simply eats an apple and ignores me. He's human, and still doesn't care a lick about what becomes of the rest of us.

"Asshole," I snarl, and he leans back. "She's not dead. You don't know that." I slam my fist on the desk. "You're all the fucking same!"

He's too stunned to say anything else as I stalk back out the huge front doors. Why does nobody care?

I should have known how this would turn out before I left home. The city guard would never lift a hand to help some small, nothing villages in the boonies.

Somebody loudly clears their throat. I turn to find the one-tusked troll standing there, arms crossed, dangling Fio's reins. If looks could kill, I'd be buried already.

I return his glare with just as much force, and for a moment, I take him by surprise. I snatch the reins out of his hands. "Thanks," I snap, and turn around to leave the way I came. He says nothing to me as I head off down the mountain.

If these assholes won't stop jerking off the Grand Chieftain long enough to help me, all while they allow the trollkin to destroy our mountain... then I'll make them pay.

JAR'KEL

That little woman's voice was so loud and annoying, I could hear the entire exchange from outside the front doors of city council.

What did she think was going to happen? That the city guard of the largest neutral city in the world would just drop everything to help a few tiny human villages? No, they're only the first stop on the wild orcs' path to the mine. If we can simply cut off the orcs at the knees, then it will help everyone.

Before she left, I should have told her that her sister is long gone now. If the wild orcs of the north are anything like the wild trolls of the jungle, she's certainly been eaten, probably while still alive. There's nothing to be done now, and trying to rescue her is a fool's errand.

But the short woman with the round face and light brown skin was determined, I'll give her that. She chewed out the unlucky fellow who works the front desk with impressive vigor. Even though she looks like a harmless little cub in her fluffy fur hood, she carries an intimidating presence.

I watch her make her way back down the mountainside, stomping her feet. At the gates, she climbs back on her... whatever it was. Pony? Large, furry dog? With big ears like those, who knows for sure.

The sun is getting lower in the sky now, and I've been told the human villages are a decent trek from here. Is she really going to walk home through the snow in the dark?

Not that it matters to me. My shift is about to start. I shrug on my corporal's coat and head down the mountain myself, but by the time I reach the bottom, the human is long gone. And this damn coat is barely protecting me from the bitter cold. I've been here for weeks now, and it still bites down to the bone.

Tonight we'll be patrolling the area near the mine, waiting for an incoming wild orc attack. The goal is to be waiting for them, with a larger force than ever before, so we can surprise them. The rest of the city guard is on standby in case the orcs decide to show themselves.

Another long, dark night of wading through this forsaken snow. As we head up higher into the mountains, toward the mine entrance, something bright and orange spills smoke into the clear sky.

"Fire!" our captain shouts. Without a second thought I pull out my sword, and then we're storming up the mountainside toward the flames licking the sky. On the way up, I spot something brown and furry far from the road, tied to a tree stump poking out of the snow. It looks familiar, like that strange beast that woman had with her before.

I don't have time for this. Soon we're at the mine, and the heat of the fire is almost welcome against the stark cold. The minecarts are in flames, but there are no wild orcs to be seen. From what I've gathered, they're not shy about showing their faces.

"Fan out!" calls the captain. "They must be here!"

While the others work on putting out the fire, I jog through the snow along a high ledge carved into the rock, where workers dump the mine carts into wagons that will bring ore back to the Grand Chieftain's empire. Maybe I'll catch whoever did this.

But there's no one out here. Damn it. Who besides wild orcs would attack the mine?

Wait. I catch a flash of gray on the slope. There's a small figure sliding down the hillside, someone with a furry hood that looks quite familiar.

It's her. The woman with the horse-dog.

"Hey!" I call out. "Stop!" But she's already reached the bottom, where her mount is waiting for her. As she climbs on, she glances up at me, and our eyes connect. Hers are small and black, shadowed by her dark, furrowed brows.

She did all this, alone?

"A human!" someone shouts, having seen her, too. "They're on the run!"

A few of us start down the road, but she's already galloping away across the snow, where she vanishes into the tall trees.

Damn. That little horse of hers sure moves fast.

SIMKA

Shit. I think he saw me.

Oh well. It's not like some idiot troll knows where I live. There are a half-dozen villages in this area, and I could be from any one of them.

It felt good to torch those mine carts. Great, even. Fuck the Grand Chieftain, and fuck his stupid mine, too. That escapade of mine was repayment. If the city guard can't be bothered to help us, then why should they help the trollkin rape our mountains for profit?

I had hoped the fire would spread to the wooden beams holding up the mine shaft, but I didn't get quite that lucky. Still, I'd done some serious damage that would take time to fix.

Everyone got what they deserved, including me. I walked away with a lightness in my heart for having gotten this speckle of revenge. It's just too bad I couldn't get away faster—I'll have to keep a low profile after this.

I face a long ride home under the shining moon, pushing Fio hard so the city guard can't catch up. I don't get back to the village until nearly sunrise, when Dad is just waking up.

"Where have you been?" he asks when I come in the front door. "You left first thing yesterday morning."

"Went after an elk," I tell him. "Led me on a wild goose chase for miles, but I didn't get him." I don't think Dad believes me, but he shrugs and goes about his morning chores anyhow. I'm exhausted from traveling all day and then all night again, so I stumble into my bedroom—the one I used to share with Vavi—and pass out cold.

It's dark outside the windows when Dad shakes me awake.

"Simka," he hisses. "What did you do?"

I jerk upright in bed. "What do you mean?"

"The Morgenzan city guard are here. They're looking for someone." He narrows his eyes. "Someone small. Human. Who tried to light the mine on fire." His voice lowers to a whisper, but his tone is still plenty severe. "It was you, wasn't it? That's where you were last night."

"Me?" I say with feigned outrage. "Why would I have done that?"

"I don't know," he growls back. "Because you're reckless." He stands back up and offers me a hand with a sigh. "Come on. They're interviewing everyone."

"Nice of them to come now," I grumble. Of course they only care when it involves the mine.

I follow Dad out of the house, toward the plaza, where all the villagers are assembled around a group of city guards, made up of humans and trollkin alike.

Unfortunately for me, the troll with broken tusk is among them. The moment I appear at the edge of the crowd, his eyes find mine. They're so foreign, with their yellow sclera and bright red irises. He frowns deeply at the sight of me, and I'm certain then that I've been found out. What's he going to do now?

Fuck. I can't end up in jail. I can't leave Dad alone.

Maybe I could say I'm one of the village hunters, and hunters are often gone for days at a time searching for big game. It's nothing unusual.

Yet, the troll doesn't speak as the other guards interrogate each of the assembled villagers about where they were last night. Most were at home, asleep, and their family members can all account for them.

When the big orc in charge finally reaches us, Dad wraps an arm around my shoulders. "We were both at home," he says. "I watched her go to bed last night."

"Fio wasn't around," chimes in the old lady who lives next door to us.

I glare at her. Traitor.

Dad sighs. "Yeah, he got out last night. We spent all morning looking for him, but the darn mule was just off digging for early grasses." It's a likely enough story, as Fio is wily and doesn't particularly like being kept in. Our neighbor huffs, and the orc quirks an eyebrow at us before accepting our excuse and moving on.

But that troll. He never takes his eyes off of me as the questioning continues. Finally, when everyone is accounted for, the captain of the city guard kicks a rock and turns back to face his men.

"We can't go on to the next village tonight, so we'll make camp here," he barks. Without even asking our village leader for permission, the guards disperse and start pulling big bundles off of their horses, setting up tents and starting campfires right in the center of town.

That should be the end of it. They didn't find what they were looking for here, so they'll go on to the next village for the next series of interviews, searching for their culprit.

"Wouldn't their time be better spent looking for the wild orcs?" I whisper to Dad as we head home.

He shushes me. "Just be glad no one identified you. I don't

know why you would do such a thing, Simka. You're only twenty-three. You have your entire life ahead of you."

I don't argue, because I know what he's not saying: I have a life ahead of me, while Vavi doesn't.

With a shake of his head, he walks off to bed and closes his door firmly.

We're both dealing with Vavi in different ways. Dad has walled himself off and built a high barrier around his heart to keep memories of her out.

I won't shut her out, though. I won't give up on her like everyone else has.

After sleeping all day, I'm anything but tired, so I slip outside to check on Fio and make sure he has plenty of grain after our long journey. I grab the shovel to muck out his pen, and I must be so lost in my thoughts that I don't notice the footsteps approaching until a pair of huge boots land in the muck on the other side of the fence.

"It's you."

My head jerks up at the deep voice. Damn it. It's the troll from earlier, with the one cracked stump of a tusk. He looks a little more well-groomed than the others, and the shiny badge on his chest makes me think he's not just some grunt like I thought. But he's not the guy in charge, either.

I stand up straight. "And who are you?" I ask.

It's stupid, I know, but he can't prove that we've met.

"Don't play games." He slides between the slats of the fence and approaches us. In response, Fio pins his ears back. He's not a big fan of strangers, and asses can be quite mean when they want to be. "I know it was you," the troll says.

If he's so certain, why didn't he turn me in? I consider throwing the shovel-full of manure I've got in my hands onto him and running for it, but I don't think I'd make it far while the village is crawling with city guards.

"You don't know anything," I say as I toss shit over the fence.

He's so tall that I have to tilt my head back quite far just to look into his eyes.

He hums and fiddles with his broken tusk. "Why did you do it? What do you have to gain?"

My anger rises like a sea serpent to the surface. I'm overwhelmed by the hurt of losing Vavi, of being turned away when I asked for help, only for the city guard to come here anyway—not to help us, of course. No, they couldn't be bothered. They're only here because I tried to burn the Grand Chieftain's precious mine down.

I whirl on him. "I did it because you are *invaders*," I snap. "What's in that mountain doesn't belong to you. And while you all are busy making your coin pockets fatter, the wild orcs are taking my people away!"

I can't read the expression on the troll's face as he simply stares at me. "You want revenge," he says mildly, then nods in understanding.

"I want my sister back!" I didn't mean it to come out so loud, and I quickly clap a hand over my mouth. His eyebrow quirks, just for a second, like my outburst amused him.

"And you're certain the wild orcs have her?"

"They took her away with them. Six months ago." I've been counting the days since then, ashamed I still haven't gotten any closer.

"Hmm." The troll's condescending calmness is annoying. "Do you know where their camp is?"

"I've been tracking them," I say. "But I haven't found it yet. I'm close, though. I know I'm close. I just... I can't get there by myself. The way is too difficult to go alone."

After a long moment of thought, the troll straightens his back.

"I'm Jar'kel," he says, and holds out his hand. "Corporal Jar'kel. Maybe we can help each other."

CHAPTER 3

JAR'KEL

The short little woman has guts, I'll give her that. She looked me right in the eye and admitted she was the one who started the fire. There's a burning need for action inside her that I haven't felt myself in some time, probably not since I lost my tusk.

"Jar'kel?" she repeats. Tentatively, she reaches out and shakes my offered hand. "I'm Simka."

"Seem-kah," I say, trying it out.

"Sih-m-ka," she corrects me.

I huff. "You're close to finding the camp, you say? You have a heading?"

"I followed their tracks when they raided the village." She points off into the snowy mountains, where the tips of the Blue Crags jut up so high they block out the moon. "I don't have a precise location yet, though. I know which direction they went, but it's treacherous up there if you don't have the right equipment.

Hell, it's treacherous even if you do. I've tried, but I can't make it all the way by myself."

I see. So she's not as certain as she led me to believe. But at least she's got an idea of where to look, and that's better than whatever the city guard have. To them, the wild orcs are like ghosts that descend from the sky when they attack, and then vanish into the mist. No one's been able to track them through these rocky, unforgiving mountains.

No one except this puny little human in her fur hood and sheepskin gloves.

"Show me," I say gruffly. If I located the camp, then we'd launch a surprise attack and take care of the problem for good. Then I could return to the desert, where I belong.

At this point, though, I wonder if the ever-present cold in my bones might be permanent, and it will follow me home.

Simka tilts her head. "Why should I show you anything?" she asks. "The city guard didn't seem so eager to help before. But suddenly you want something from me? Now that I have information?"

I take a step toward her, but she doesn't back away. She gives me a dirty look, like she's daring me to pick a fight. I only mean to seem threatening when I lean down close to her, but as I inhale, I get a hearty whiff of her. She smells like pine trees and snow, with just a hint of animal. That hides what's underneath: something warm, soft, and full of life. Bursting at the seams with vibrance.

"I want to end this fight," I growl. "I want to find them, so we can be done with all the bullshit and I can go home."

She blinks. "Go home?"

"Back to where I belong. Somewhere that isn't this frozen hellscape." I spit on the ground, as if to show the snow just how I feel about it.

"Huh." Simka doesn't seem perturbed by the fact I'm towering over her, shadowing the light of the moon on her face. She rubs her chin. "And you're willing to act without permission by your superiors?"

I bark out a laugh. "If it's for the city guard, all will be forgiven." No one would question how I discovered the camp's location if I brought it back to the commander. "Now show me. Where did they go?"

The wheels turn in her mind. She's weighing her options, deciding whether or not to trust me.

"You said you wanted help, and here it is," I tell her. "We find them, then the city guard jumps them in the middle of the night. And if your sister is still alive, I'll make sure you get her back." I hold out my hand. "Sound like a deal?"

Simka narrows her eyes as she studies me. They're small and dark as the night, but they have a shine in them that tells me she might just accept my offer. She's a rebel, a free thinker. I can use that.

"Fine." Simka takes my hand in hers. She has five fingers, but they're so small they can only wrap around two of my four. We clasp hands and shake. "I'll give you what I know. But you're going to need some better equipment."

She leaves me there as she returns to her house. After some time waiting—while her little mongrel steed gives me the side-eye—Simka returns with a pile of pelts in her arm. She tosses a big one at me. "Put this on. Your blue skin is going to stand out like a sore thumb. Plus, you look like you could use something a little... warmer."

The damn human isn't wrong. Despite my pride, I take the fur and find it's more of a cloak. It wraps around my shoulders and ties under my chin, keeping my arms and back quite warm. It's small, like she is, but it's a marked improvement.

"Fine." I pull the hood up over my head, and immediately the tips of my long ears feel cozy and warm, probably for the first time since I arrived in this awful place. "Lead the way, *Simka*."

SIMKA

So the troll wants to work together.

That's what I'd asked for when I went to the city guard for help. But there's just one of him and one of me—not at all the force I'd been hoping for. We'll need more than just the two of us if we're going to take on an entire clan of wild orcs.

Still, this is a step forward. If he's right, and we bring the exact location of the camp back with us, then the city guard can act. Corporal Jar'kel gave me his word that he'd make sure Vavi got out safely. He's a straightforward kind of person, who has so far told the ugly truth right to my face rather than lie about it.

I decide not to bring Fio along because the high-up cliffs are much too steep for him to climb, and I don't want to leave him at the base when we reach it. Who knows how long we'll be up there? After I've packed up some food and supplies, I find my dad's pair of snowshoes and write him a note.

"I'm going after Vavi," I scribble. "This is my best shot at finding her. I'm sorry." I just have to hope I make it back safely, because I don't know what would become of Dad if he lost both his daughters.

Jar'kel gives the snowshoes a skeptical look. "You want me to wear these... plates on my feet?"

"They're not plates. Look. They're lightweight." I wave one around in the air. "I made these myself, and I promise they're solid." Even for a creature his size, they should keep him from falling through the snow.

His brow furrows. "You *made* them?"

"Yup. Just like I made that cloak you're wearing." I pull out a pair of mittens that may or may not fit him. I made them for Dad years ago, but they were too big. "And these, too."

Jar'kel eyes them like they're a small animal with sharp teeth. He slips on one mitten, and I don't miss the flicker of pleasure in his eyes when it fits. They're leather on the outside and soft fur on the inside, which should keep his strange, four-fingered hands warm as we hike up the mountain.

"Huh." He flexes his fingers, testing them out—but he doesn't say anything else, not even a cursory "thank you." I huff and start off, weaving behind houses so no one sees us, and we can avoid the soldiers camped in the plaza. I sling my snowshoes over my back, because we won't need them until we reach the higher altitudes where the snowfall is too heavy to walk through.

Jar'kel follows me as we head off into the trees in the direction I tracked the wild orcs after they took Vavi. We hike through the dark woods in silence, only the light of the stars and moon guiding our way. There's no conversation to make between us. He's trollkin and I'm human, and we have nothing in common. No, he's just another trespasser, sent from some desert far down south.

When we reach the first slope, I stop to put on my snowshoes. I have to show Jar'kel how to strap in his feet, and he struggles with it after refusing my help.

"Don't be so stubborn," I say, kneeling down in front of him to put them on properly. "You can admit that you don't know what you're doing."

He simply grunts and lets me finish. Once he's ready, we start trekking again. His steps are slow and awkward at first as he tries to get used to the snow shoes.

"Just walk normally," I tell him. "I know the extra weight is strange, but you'll go faster if you try."

Again, he responds with a grunt. I roll my eyes as we get moving again.

It's still a slow climb up the mountain. We hike and hike until the dark sky begins to lighten at the edges, fading from a deep blue to a light purple. I love the way the sunrise tickles the surface of the snow, making it glitter. Once the sun has fully emerged from over the top of the mountains, I stop at a large boulder to take off my pack and pull out some food.

"Won't the city guard miss you when they wake up and find you gone?" I ask Jar'kel, hoping for at least a smidgen of conversation. "Will they come looking for you?"

He shrugs. "They won't spare the soldiers for that. We just have to focus on finding the camp right now."

I sigh and chew some of my jerky. It's too bad that I got stuck with such a grump. Life as a hunter—or a hunter-in-training—can get rather boring, and I thought having a companion for once would be nice.

Guess not.

When we're done eating, we resume our hike. Jar'kel's pace has picked up as he's gotten used to wearing the snowshoes, and we're making decent progress. With another body here, we can haul our packs up the mountain together and finally reach the leg of the journey I haven't been able to attempt alone.

When we arrive at the base of the icy cliff, we come to a stop. Jar'kel gazes up the stretch of blue ice, then he turns to me with his mouth hanging open.

"We have to climb this?" he asks, horrified.

"Yup." I pull out my ice picks and rope. "I'll go first. After that, you send our packs up. You'll go up last so I can hold your rope. Okay?"

"I can't believe this," Jar'kel mutters under his breath. "I'm going to die out here."

I pat his arm. "You probably won't. And if you do, you'll fall such a long way that you'll die instantly. No pain, you know."

He gives me an incredulous look as I stand up tall and bury my pick in the ice. One step after another, I climb my way up, the rope unwinding the higher I get. We're in full daylight now, and the ice sparkles under the sunlight.

As dangerous as it is, I love it up here in the mountains. You can see everything, from the high walls of Morgenzan to the east, all the way to the farthest human villages in the west. The might of the Blue Crags is displayed in all its majesty, like huge teeth jutting high up into the sky. They are not meant to be tamed, to be pillaged and plundered. They are meant to be admired and feared.

I wonder if this grumpy troll can appreciate that. Probably not. I don't think he appreciates much of anything.

Chapter 4

JAR'KEL

I did not expect how fearful I'd feel watching this tiny slip of a human climb her way up the wall of sheer ice. She could fall at any time. If one of her picks gave way, she would tumble down to her death far below.

And yet still she ascends, one step at a time, high above me. From here, her heavy winter coat no longer covers her small, pert rear. Each time she moves her legs, it flexes one strong, rounded cheek. Her hide pants are tight, too, leaving very little to the imagination.

To my absolute horror, the clear view shoots a bolt of lightning from my throat down into my groin. After a decade of somber sleep, my cock lifts its head, curious about this new development. I smother it with my hand, absolutely enraged that it would decide at this moment to make itself known.

To be honest, I thought my desire had fully vanished when Pa'zi and I chose to go our separate ways. My cock hadn't hungered for her in some time anyway, and rarely does it even call for my attention. Occasionally when I can't sleep, I take it in hand and hurriedly pump out a release, but even the need for that has faded over time. I expected that would be the case until the day I died.

Which could be today. And still, looking death in the face, my traitorous dick has decided this tiny human is rather appealing.

Her perfect ass curls as her strong thighs reach for the next foothold. I wonder what that ass would feel like against my hand if it were bare.

Up above I hear a gasp as one of Simka's feet slips on the ice. I imagine her tumbling to her death, and a warning rises in my throat... but she doesn't fall. Still, I find my arms are held out already, ready to catch her, as if there's any sense in that. There's not a chance I could cushion her landing.

But the higher she climbs, the greater my anxiety grows. It would be a shame if her life ended here. She's young and hardy, and her heart is set firmly on rescuing her sister, which I have to admit I find admirable.

At long last, Simka crests the peak and climbs up onto stable ground. A relieved breath escapes my lips. She crows loudly from the top, and the shock of sound takes me by surprise. When she glances down at me and waves, I find myself waving back. She made it alive.

"Now send up the packs," Simka shouts. She ties a rope around a solid rock at her feet, then tosses down the other end to me. Obeying her instructions—she is the expert here, after all, and even I can acknowledge that—I tie the rope around both our packs and tug on it to let her know they're ready. She gathers the rope, pulling it up one stroke at a time. I thought I'd have to carry everything up with us, but this clever little human had a plan all along.

When she's finally retrieved our bags, Simka tosses the rope down to me once again. "You're too big for me to pull up," she calls from her high perch. "Step back. I'm throwing the picks down."

What? She expects me to climb up the ice the way she did? I

have no experience whatsoever. I thought she was going to haul me up like the luggage.

"Don't worry," she hastily adds. "Tie the rope around your waist. If you slip, I won't let you die. Or I'll try my best. Okay?"

I can't believe this. But I have a purpose here, so when the pick axes come tumbling down, I fish them out of the snow and test them out in the ice. It takes me a few attempts, but I manage to sink the points deeply enough that they'll support my weight.

"Take it slow," Simka calls. "One foot at a time."

Grumbling, I do what she says. I bury the tip of one pick in the ice, test it to make sure it's firmly planted, and then repeat with the other pick. I make my way slowly, probably only a fraction of Simka's speed, up the sheer wall. I'm holding myself up with just my arms and my feet braced against the surface, and I'm only halfway to the top when my muscles start to grow tired.

Then I make the mistake of looking down. The sheet of ice is bottomless, the ground so far below me that it's a sin against nature.

"No, Jar'kel!" Simka shouts. "Keep going! Don't stop for a second." Her voice is so commanding that my military training makes me obey without thinking twice. I continue my way up, one ice pick at a time, trying not to ponder the terrible, empty distance between me and the snowpack far below. My heart is pounding and my arms are screaming for relief as I near the top, where Simka clutches the rope tight. She won't let me fall, I'm sure of it.

No one has ever made me feel sure I wouldn't fall.

Then, at last, I'm at the top. I crawl over the cliff's edge, collapsing to my knees as I take huge breaths to refill my lungs. Simka stands over me with her hands on her hips, smiling widely.

"Well, you did it, mister troll." She offers me a hand to help me up, and I take it without thinking. "Good job."

My blood warms, but whether it's due to her praise, or relief that I made it up here alive, I'm not sure.

SIMKA

Well, Jar'kel didn't die. That's a good start. He's in great physical shape, and he kept his cool, even that far off the ground.

Now that we're up here, I have a much clearer view of what we face ahead. I've never ventured this far from home, so I don't have a perfect map in my mind of where the orc camp might be. We'll just have to search in the general direction their prints were headed until we find traces of them.

"Where to?" the corporal asks, getting to his feet next to me. This close up, he blocks out the sun just like the jagged mountain peaks do.

I shrug. "Not sure. I've never gotten this far before."

He flashes me an incredulous look. "You can't be serious. You don't know?" He curses under his breath. "Should have never trusted a human."

"Hey! Since when were the city guard ever going to get this far? You didn't have a clue where to look before you met me." I gesture out at the snowy slopes ahead of us. Here there's a clear path through the ridges and crevasses, between two towering peaks. "They can't be much farther, and there's only one way to go. We'll keep looking until we find them." I'm optimistic now that we've made it to the top. With both our sets of eyes on the job, surely we'll have a much better shot at this.

Jar'kel rubs his forehead, smoothing out the creases between his brows. I wonder what sorts of things he's seen and done in his life that have made him so hard and bitter on the outside.

I start off, pack over my shoulder, snowshoes strapped to my feet once more. This time the troll keeps pace with me. He's got good stamina, too. I don't know much about how trollkin age, but by the creases in his face and the way the blue of his hair is fading at the tips, he looks like he could be as old as my father.

Still, there's something about his strong jaw and broad shoulders that turns my cheeks warm when I look at him. I like the concentrated frown he wears as he focuses on taking one step after another. If he keeps up this speed, we should make decent progress before night falls.

We hike over snow-covered ridges, down into small valleys and back up again. When we reach a sudden cliff, there's only one place the camp could be.

"There," I say, pointing. "It has to be across the pass." Two mountains connect here, but the terrain is uneven and treacherous. The sun is dropping lower in the sky now, casting long, dusky shadows. "We should stop for the night."

Jar'kel balks. "Stop? We still have plenty of daylight."

"It'll be dark by the time we get over there," I gesture at the narrow path that leads to the next slope, "and we don't want to try to navigate that without good light."

With an indignant grumble, he pulls off his pack. Each of us brought a bedroll along with our food supplies, so we sit down and eat what we can as the sun sets. Jar'kel doesn't make conversation with me, but just having another presence around is comforting. I've been searching these mountains alone for so long that it's a welcome relief just to have another presence nearby.

I clear away snow to make a pit, and dig some small logs out of my pack. There's no wood up here this high above the tree line, so this is all we have, but it will be nice to get warm after such a long day.

When I start the fire, Jar'kel moves closer and holds out his hands in front of it. I study him in the low light, how the sharp downward curve of his mouth has left harsh dimples. Maybe I was wrong about him being ugly. He has a big, regal nose that matches his stern brows. The color of his blue hair is wild, much unlike his personality. How did he grow up? What brought him under the employ of the city guard?

"Your Freysian is good," I remark as we eat. He quirks an eyebrow at me.

"Of course it is. It's my job to talk to humans."

"Why?" I tilt my head. "I mean, why did you join the city guard?"

He tears off a piece of his elk jerky—which I gave him, by the way, and he still hasn't thanked me. "You don't need to know that," he says. "All we're here for is to find this camp. That's it." His tone is sharp and final.

A seed of hurt settles inside me. "You're kind of an asshole," I say.

Jar'kel's eyebrows jump into his hair, but his expression quickly morphs into a scowl. "I'm glad you think so," he says. "Maybe then you'll stop talking so much." He gets to his feet and finds his way to his pack, then pulls out his bedroll and spreads it out over the snow. Without any further fanfare, or even a *good-night*, he climbs in and turns his back toward me.

I'd thought we might be companions in this mission, but he's told me in no uncertain terms that we aren't. I'm just a convenient vehicle for him to get what he wants.

But isn't that what he is for me, too? He's just helping me to find Vavi, and then we'll be done with each other.

I let the fire burn as I retrieve my own rolled-up furs and lay them out. But it's hard to fall asleep, even under the stars where I feel most at home, thinking about Jar'kel's scowl and what it might look like if he smiled, instead.

JAR'KEL

I probably shouldn't be so mean to her, but I don't like the tingling sensation I get in my belly when I look at her over the fire. Her sharp, midnight eyes reflect the flames as she stares into them, the fur rim of her hood framing her small, round face. She looks fierce, competent and confident. She's someone who can take care of herself and doesn't require coddling, and I find myself admiring it.

I can't think like that. I need to cut this off at the bud, whatever it is, and give it no room to spread. She's human. I've already seen what happens when trollkin like me fall for humans, and it's ugly and messy. Both my captain and lieutenant hung up their soldiers' coats to be together.

Not to mention that she's much, much too young. She doesn't truly understand life yet—I can see that much in her optimism. She still thinks she can mold the world into the shape she wants it to be, and hasn't accepted yet that we are both simply cogs in a much larger machine.

But the look on her face when I told her to fuck off? I felt like a bit of a bastard. Still, I have to remember this is an arrangement of convenience and strategy. I'll learn what I need to learn, bring it back to the commander and the city council, and once the threat is dealt with, I'll finally be free to go back home. That's all I want out of this.

Still, as I try to fall asleep, I can't stop picturing Simka climbing up the ice above me, her fur coat flaring out to reveal her small, pert butt. My cock awakens at the memory, and I curse under my breath. What's inside those sheepskin pants? No, not just there. Everywhere. She's tough as leather on the outside, but I think she would be small and soft inside that fur coat.

Damn it. It's been ages since I felt the need to pump one out, but now my cock is at full mast under my pants. Not that I can take care of it here, right across the fire from Simka. I squash my eyes closed and take deep breaths, willing my cursed dick to go down.

It takes me ages to fall asleep, long past the moment when Simka's breathing has turned even and slow. As much as I try to banish it, I keep remembering her high up in the air, each muscle working as she climbed an impossible height, trying to save her sister.

I awaken to find Simka already up and chewing her breakfast in the dim morning light. Her eyes dart to me when I rise from my bedroll, and then fall back to the remains of the fire. Hopefully, we'll find what we're looking for early in the day, so we can go home without having to spend yet another frigid night out here.

I never want to see snow again as long as I live.

Simka doesn't speak to me as we pack up. She is as hard as the ice on the outside, having taken my reprimand to heart.

Good. Then we should have no more conflict on this trip.

We set off across the pass early, and it's just as treacherous as she promised. I have to pause a few times and collect myself when I see the cliffside looming below me, where all it would take is one misstep to go tumbling down to my death. Simka leads the way, steady and sure on her feet. I follow in the light tracks left behind by her snow shoes, certain that if I keep to her path, I won't die up here. She might be small, but she's also strong, and she never seems to tire. Once, she glances back as if to check on me, then hardens her face and returns to the hike.

Finally, she reaches the top of the ridge. Simka turns to me, eyes wide, and gestures for me to come look. Her face is radiant.

I jog the rest of the way up the hill to see what it is she's found. Below us, the wild orc camp sprawls like a mold, having taken over most of the hollowed-out valley. The dozens of tents are protected from the winds by the surrounding hills and cliffs, which I envy right now as the blistering cold bites my skin.

"Found it," Simka breathes, a huge smile on her face. I like how it squeezes her round cheeks and crinkles her eyes.

I almost pat her on the back. That's all I needed. Now, if we can just return safely the way we came, I can pass the location on to the commander, and we'll make sure Simka's sister is safe. I owe her that much for getting me here.

"Halt!" a deep, booming voice shouts in Trollkin. Simka spins around in surprise, snatching her dagger from her belt. An orc emerges from behind a large boulder, dressed in leather and furs, his hair long and braided. A necklace made of fangs hangs from his neck. He's not alone, either. Another orc steps out behind him, equally large and also armed.

How did they get past both of us? How did we not notice we weren't alone?

When I reach for my own sword, an arrow whistles through the air. It lands in the snow right next to my feet—a clear warning. Another orc stands high up above us, her next arrow ready.

Damn it. There's my chance of going home, up in smoke.

CHAPTER 5

SIMKA

Jar'kel doesn't speak to me as we're bound by the wrists with leather ties and dragged down the snowy slope toward the camp. What's there to say? This whole mission was for nothing.

The orcs all speak in Trollkin, so I can't understand them. Damn it. I wish I knew what we were walking into, but Jar'kel keeps silent and doesn't even try to translate for me. By the look on his face, though, I don't think what they're saying is good.

Vavi. I failed her, and I failed Dad, too. Now there will be nothing left for him at home, and he'll have yet another daughter to mourn.

The camp is populated by hardy tents made of deer hide, the roofs held up with wood posts. It bustles with activity, orcs going this way and that. I keep my fear and my dread all bottled up, and instead put on a carefully neutral face. As we're led through rows and rows of tents, Jar'kel doesn't raise his head once. The orcs call to others as they pass, exchanging grunts and laughs. Our leather ties are jerked as we're shown off. Will they kill us, or will they keep us alive to wring some entertainment from us first?

There's a great open area in the center of the camp with a huge fire pit dug in the middle, and wooden trestle tables assembled around it. There, they throw both of us to the ground.

I find myself looking at a pair of bare green feet, the four toes wrapped with leather that trails up the ankle. Wolfskin pants hug the calf, and I chance a look up at the owner.

He's huge, bigger than any orc I've ever seen, with long hair hanging down his shoulders. His face is brutish, with a nose that was once surely broken, and two massive tusks curving up from his jutting jaw. His eyes are yellow and cruel, and I know that I won't be leaving this place alive.

There's an "oof!" as Jar'kel is hurled down onto the ground next to me. Again the orc growls something in Trollkin, and Jar'kel lifts his head, eyes ablaze, and snaps something back at him— something I'm certain will get us both killed.

"Shut up," I hiss. Then the massive orc gestures to two others standing at his flanks and they grab our ropes, hauling us back to our feet.

"What did you say?" I snarl at Jar'kel.

"I told him not to delay it."

"Delay what?" Then it occurs to me: this idiot troll asked them to kill us quickly. "You jackass!" I could just spit on his face. "You've sentenced us to death!"

"A fast death is better than a slow one," he says. "You know, even though we ended up here—" the orcs snatch up our ropes again and yank us along behind them— "you're an interesting girl, Simka."

"Interesting?!" I could claw his eyes out. "That's the best you can do?" I can't believe I'm going to die alongside this asshole.

"Simka?" The sound of a familiar voice floats from behind me. I glance around, sure that I've imagined it—but then I find a familiar woman running up to us. Jet-black hair flutters around her slender face, and her big dark eyes are wide and disbelieving.

It's my sister. And she's *alive*.

"V-Vavi?" I whisper. I'm frozen to the spot. "Is that really you?"

"Wait! Gorren, let her go!" Vavi waves her hands back and forth to get the big orc's attention. "That's my sister!"

Our captors halt, and I take the chance to get to my feet—only to be bowled over by Vavi. It's her, as sure as the sun is bright. She wraps her arms around me and brings me in close.

She's always been good at giving hugs. I bury my face in her shoulder, and even though she smells different than I remember, I never want her to let me go.

"Sister?" the orc's deep voice booms in a familiar language. He speaks our tongue? Vavi releases me, and he approaches her from behind, casually running a hand through her long hair. "This is Vavi's sister?"

"Yes!" Vavi shrieks, and I also forgot how loud she can be. "Oh my gosh, Simka. What are you doing here?"

It takes me a moment to lift my jaw up off the ground. "I'm looking for you," I say. She isn't bound up with leather ties, like we are. She's standing freely at this orc's side, one of his hands looped over her shoulder, and she's dressed in the same leathers and furs that he is.

Vavi's face falls. "Oh. You shouldn't have come." Next to me, the corporal's jerked to his feet by our captors, and he stumbles in the snow. I hope they don't hurt him.

"Why not?" I ask, perplexed. "Of course I would come looking for you." My lip trembles from the sheer relief I feel at seeing her well again.

Vavi shakes her head with deep regret. "The camp is hard to find for a reason." She glances at Jar'kel and her expression grows even darker. "And who's this?"

"Corporal Jar'kel," I say. "He's with the city guard." Jar'kel snarls and makes a cutting gesture across his throat.

Ah, shit, I guess I shouldn't have said that.

"City guard?" the orc says, baring his teeth.

Vavi looks increasingly distraught. "And he's here looking for our camp as well?"

"*Our* camp?" I repeat. What does she mean? She's not one of them, one of these *orcs*.

Vavi nods, and places one of her hands over Gorren's. He visibly relaxes. "Ours," she answers in a steady voice.

She can't possibly be saying what I think she's saying. These monsters came and kidnapped her. They *stole* her, right from our home.

"Who is this guy, Vavi?" I gesture at the orc who still has one arm around her.

"He's the leader of the clan," she says, rubbing her hand over his. "And I'm his mate."

I stare at her, my mind going blank. "Mate?" I echo. I only know what this means in the context of the arctic hawks, who mate for life.

She raises her eyes to his, affection plain on her face. "Yes. I'm his everything, and he's mine. We were bound together, fated to find each other by..." She trails off. "By a higher power." Gorren's hand travels down her body to the swell at her hips, where she cups her own hand over it. "And," Vavi says with a hint of a grin, "I'm going to be having his baby pretty soon. Or whelp. Whatever you want to call it."

This must be a dream. A really weird, fucked up dream that I'm only having because I've been chasing Vavi's shadow for so long.

Wait, no. It's a nightmare. Definitely a nightmare.

"There's no way," I whisper. "That's not true." There's no way my sister believes this.

But Vavi nods rapidly. "It is true! And oh, Simka, it's the best thing to ever happen to me." She smiles up at the monstrous, terrifying orc, and to my surprise, he smiles back at her. The expression is odd and unpracticed, but it's genuine, and directed right at my sister.

She isn't lying. She's "mated" to this beast, whatever that means. And she's so pregnant that it must have happened the moment she came here.

I can't believe what I'm seeing. All this time that she's been gone, all this time that we've missed her, and she was up here shacking up with a fucking orc?

Vavi glances at Jar'kel. "Why is he here with you? Is he a friend of yours, Simka?"

"He..." I begin, not sure what to say. He's made it clear we aren't friends, but I'm not sure that's the right answer right now.

Gorren spits on the ground. "City guard are not welcome here. The troll will die."

"What?!" I gape at Vavi. "You can't kill him!"

Jar'kel, though, appears totally unfazed by this. "Expected as much." He cracks me a sideways smile. "But I'm glad you have an in."

As the orcs start to drag him away, I grab onto Vavi's arm. "Wait, wait! You can't!" I turn a pleading gaze on her. "What's going on here? Please, Vavi, don't let them do this."

"I'm sorry, Simka," she says, rubbing my shoulder, but I shove her away. "But no one can know that we're here. Especially not the city guard. He can't be allowed to live with what he knows."

Jar'kel simply nods, and the two orcs holding him by the arms resume their march. But I can't just let him die. I'm the only reason we're here in the first place. I have to save him somehow.

Taking one more look at Jar'kel, with his one stubby tusk, his face relaxing as he resigns himself to his fate, I make a split-second decision.

"Wait." I glare at the woman who used to be my sister, who

must have been replaced with someone else when she was stolen from our home. "He's... he's mine, Vavi." I lower my voice, hoping I can really sell it. "He's *my* mate."

Vavi blinks, and Gorren's eyes go wide. Jar'kel gives me a puzzled expression, like I've just spoken in a language he doesn't understand.

"What?" Vavi whispers, disbelieving. Her eyes go wide and bright, and she rushes towards me, taking my hands in hers. "So you've felt it, too? The mating bond?"

I nod vigorously. "Yes. I have. *We* have."

Jar'kel looks simply aghast. "We're n—" he begins, and I cut him off.

"It's amazing, isn't it?" I say, even more earnestly. I can't believe I'm doing this, but it's his only chance. "The, um... the bond."

"Yes!" Vavi cries, throwing her arms around me so her big belly squeezes between us. "There's nothing else like it." When she releases me she returns to Gorren, leaning in close to him. He hungrily rubs his hands over her body, up to her breasts. She doesn't even seem to mind as he gropes her in front of us. In fact, she sighs with pleasure.

"I'm so glad you've found it, too, Simka," Vavi goes on. She bats her eyelashes at Gorren. "We can't kill him, my love. The troll is my sister's mate. That means he's safe, right?"

The big orc studies me and Jar'kel suspiciously.

"You wouldn't kill my sister's mate," Vavi repeats, uncertainty in her voice. "Just don't let them go. They'll stay here, with us, and no one will ever learn that we're here." She turns back to me. "Right, Simka? If the clan doesn't kill him, you won't try to leave, right? It's really lovely here, where you're accepted. You'll see."

I hold up both hands. "I want to be where you are, Vavi," I say. "Of course I do."

She smiles again, and by the expression on Gorren's face, I can tell he's already given in.

"Fine," he growls. "The troll will not die." Gorren waves off the two orcs holding Jar'kel captive, saying something imperious in Trollkin, and they untie the ropes around our wrists.

Vavi claps her hands together. "Oh, this will be the best thing ever," she says, radiating pure joy. "You found your own mate with a trollkin, too! We really are cut from the same cloth." She gives me a gentle push towards Jar'kel. "Now you can be together, without anyone looking down on you. Your relationship is celebrated here." She winks conspiratorially. "There are others like us among the clan, you know."

"Others?" I ask.

"You know. Humans and orcs. *Mates.*"

"Right." I shoot a sideways glance at Jar'kel, and Vavi's grin fades.

"What's wrong?" she asks. "Shouldn't you be... happier?"

Oh. I realize then what she's asking. She expects me to crawl all over the corporal the way she's basically melded into this big, ugly orc.

"Of course I am. I'm just... surprised, that's all. And we're so used to, you know, keeping it a secret." I sidle up to Jar'kel, who's watching me from the corner of his eye, and slide an arm around his waist. "We're very happy we can be ourselves here. Aren't we?"

He finally seems to catch my meaning. With a grunt, he awkwardly hugs me against his side in return. I turn my head up towards his.

"Kiss me," I whisper, so quietly I hope Vavi can't hear me.

He looks into my eyes, uncertain. His lip twitches, and then, quite suddenly, he captures my chin in his hand. He leans down so my face is cradled between his tusks, and plants his lips firmly on mine.

CHAPTER 6

JAR'KEL

It's for the cause—the cause of staying alive.

That's what I tell myself as I take Simka's mouth. Her lips are perfectly soft, and she tastes like the dried berries she ate for breakfast. If I want to live, I need to sell it, so I curl both arms around her and pull her in close, bending as far down as I can to reach her while she stands up on her toes. Uncertainly, her hands slide around my neck, but soon she returns my fervor, her lips parting for my tongue.

Surely I don't need to do that to make this ruse effective. But as I sink into her, the less this becomes about saving my own skin and the more it becomes about tasting her and drinking her in. Her mouth is so pliable under mine, but her lips are also fierce as they learn their way around me.

Shit, she's good at this.

When I pull away suddenly, Simka opens her eyes, looking dazed. She blinks a few times at me, confused. Then she clears her throat, as if realizing for the first time we have an audience, and steps away from me.

"Oh!" Her sister, Vavi, is simply over the moon. She looks much like Simka, but with a pointier chin and longer hair. She's also all smiles, where Simka rarely doles them out. "I'm so happy for you. Welcome to the clan, sis. And you!" She grins widely at me, showing both rows of white, blunt teeth. "Thank you, corporal. For taking care of my sister when I couldn't."

Simka's done a plenty good job taking care of herself, but I don't know what to say that won't give me away as a liar, so I only nod.

"A man of few words," she says with a wink. "Troll, I mean."

Vavi turns to her orc mate and whispers something in his ear, her hand linking with his. Humans and trollkin mating, among this clan of barbarians? I'm mystified by it. The more I search the crowd, the more humans I see among them with their orc companions. There's something going on here, something I don't understand yet. Why would there be this bastion of trollkin-human relationships contained in this one camp of brigands?

Perhaps I'll find out.

"You," the clan leader says, pointing at me, and then at Simka. His grasp of Freysian is surprisingly good, though thickly accented. "A tent is prepared for you." Then he turns to his mate, a hand grazing over her belly. There's no question in my mind that he feels the mating bond, if this is how he's behaving. "We leave now."

The two of them scurry away, and an orcess wearing a long leather dress with fur-cuffed edges gestures for us to follow her. Simka takes my hand with a significant look. I accept it, because I don't have a choice, and hold it loosely in mine as we follow behind her. Her fingers are so small that the entirety of her hand fits into my palm.

Though she's so slight, I'm comforted by her sturdy touch. Once again, Simka didn't let me fall.

We're led to a tent in the center of the camp, and more wild orcs are already there, sweeping it out and carrying in wood. The orcess shows us inside, where a fire is being built in the center of the tent, and a bed full of soft furs lies in the back.

"This is where you and your mate will stay," she tells me in Trollkin, and like the clan leader, it's in an odd dialect I've never heard before. The fire is lit from a torch, and then the wild orcs leave us, letting the flap fall closed behind them.

Now, we're alone.

I sit down on the furs and drop my head in my hands. I can finally take a moment to think about where we find ourselves. Simka has sentenced us to a difficult fate with her lie. She sinks into the furs near me, keeping a polite distance between us.

"I can't believe you did that," I mutter.

She scowls. "I saved your life! They'd have cut off your head, or whatever it is they do here."

"Nobody asked you. Death is unpleasant, but I've made my peace with it." I've accepted the truth of my own mortality ever since the bandit attack in the desert.

Simka's mouth falls open. "You'd rather I let them kill you?" She shakes her head in disbelief. "Maybe I should have."

All I can do is nod. Lucky for me, escape is still possible. The next time the orcs leave for a coordinated attack, I'll make my getaway. And if they catch me... I'll accept whatever comes.

"It was a wasted effort," I tell her.

Simka doesn't speak as more orcs appear with food. We eat in silence, and I watch from the corner of my eye as Simka devours her roasted venison. She has so much life in her, it's ridiculous that anyone believed her story. I would never be mated to someone so fresh and energetic.

When she's finished, Simka finally speaks. "I still can't believe it." She wipes off her mouth with one hand. "My sister is married to an orc. Or mated. Whatever." Her eyes travel up to the hole in the top of the tent, where the smoke from the fire escapes. "It doesn't make sense, but also makes perfect sense. Why they were stealing young people from the villages. They're *looking* for mates."

This baffles me as well. I thought cross-species mating was limited to my former captain and her orc lieutenant, who served in the Attirex city guard alongside me. I thought it was a strange, once-in-a-lifetime event when they both vacated their posts to be together, but now I'm faced with the idea it's more widespread than that.

These orcs, far outside of the rest of trollkin civilization, have not only accepted the concept, but embraced it. They seem to be seeking it out.

"Why?" Simka asks again, and I'm not sure if she's talking to me or herself. "Why would they want humans?"

"Perhaps to preserve their civilization." I finish my own meal and set the tray aside on the floor where I'm sitting. "Trollkin and humans can reproduce. I've seen it. Perhaps their numbers have dwindled so much they were forced to look elsewhere for mates."

Simka blinks. "My sister *is* pregnant. And she didn't have any relationships when she was taken."

I nod. This supports my theory.

"Damn it." She leans forward on the bed, dropping her face into her hands. "We can't leave. And neither can she. Not that she even cares to, which I still don't understand. Surely she would want to see Dad again. And me." Her voice trembles. "Vavi would have wanted to tell me she was okay, right?"

I don't know what to say. Simka's sister seems happy here, as strange as it is, and I don't know why she wouldn't want her sister to be happy. But I haven't had family since I was young, so perhaps I simply don't understand.

When I don't answer, Simka sits back up and puts on a tough face. "Fine. Don't say anything."

I shrug. "I don't know what you want me to say."

"Ugh!" She crawls into the bed, pulling the furs over herself, and turns away from me. "Goodnight, Jar'kel. I hope you like sleeping on the floor."

Getting the hint, I take one of the furs rolled up in the corner of the tent and spread it out in front of the fire. At least it's warm here, and I'm still alive.

Though lying on the bed next to Simka's small body... perhaps that would have been warmer. Certainly softer. But this is how it'll be, until the moment I can make my escape.

SIMKA

I didn't hate Jar'kel at first. It was more like a begrudging companionship, where we tolerated each other for a singular goal. He'd kept my transgression at the mine a secret, and I owed him for that, at least.

Now I'm pretty sure I hate him. How can anyone be so emotionless? It's like nothing matters to him, not even his own life.

We're truly trapped here now. If we try to run, they'll kill us. If we stay, we're stuck here forever. I'll never see Dad again, and that fills my heart with an aching, creeping dread.

I was young when Mom died. A fever came through the village, and when she fell sick, Vavi and I were moved to another house. Dad did his best to care for her without catching it himself, but the sickness was too much for her, and she passed in the night.

I don't remember her the way Vavi does. Our mother is like a ghost in my mind, a figure with no face that speaks words with no voice. I know that she loved me, but beyond that, my memory of her is an empty space.

Now we'll leave Dad with nothing and no one. When I'm sure that Jar'kel's asleep, I let a few of the tears that have been building up behind my eyes fall. I'm trapped here now, forced to pretend I'm in love with a troll who clearly detests me. For how long? For the rest of my life?

I choke on my tears as they flow faster. Damn it. If I let this feeling take over it will rule me, and I'll never get through this. I have to steel myself against it the way I've learned to steel myself against the cold. Bundle up tighter, clench your teeth, and hope that eventually you find a fire.

But the tears won't stop, and I try to muffle my sounds with my hand. The last thing I need is for the corporal to catch me this way, pathetic and weak. No, I need to match his coolness with my own. Pretend he doesn't get under my skin. Pretend that it didn't hurt when he laid down on the floor and chose to sleep by the fire instead, even though I'm the one who told him off.

Unfortunately, there's nothing to do about it. So I bury my face in the furs, hoping eventually my body will tire itself out.

"Simka." Jar'kel's voice startles me.

"What?" I snap, trying not to let the fact I've been crying seep into my voice.

"You're keeping me awake."

"Well, sorry, but I can't help it! I mean, this is the rest of our lives, and we can't leave. How are you not more upset?"

I hear him shifting, and he sits up in his makeshift bed. "Because I don't intend to stay like you do."

I rub the tears out of my eyes with my fists. "They'll never let us go. You heard Vavi and Gorren. Their location is a secret, and now that we know it—"

"You're going to let that stop you?" He huffs with condescension. "I didn't think you were the type to hand in your resignation so soon. But I'm going to find a way out."

I sit up, too, and stare down at him open-mouthed. "You can't be serious. They'll kill you if they catch you trying to run."

"Then I won't let them catch me." He lowers his eyebrows.

"The moment you give up, you lose." With those final words, he lies down and rolls over to face the dying fire.

I wonder if he's right. Is there really a way out of here, or is that a recipe for getting our heads cut off after all? If Vavi is as attached to Gorren as I think she is, she won't go with us. And if the wild orcs catch us running, even being Vavi's sister might not save me.

I pull the furs close, trying to shut my eyes and keep them that way. But I feel even more alone than ever, sentenced to this tent with Jar'kel, living a stupid lie I told.

Escaping. I would hate to leave Vavi here, but then at least I could get back to Dad and let him know we're all right. But then the city guard will come and invade the camp, and who knows what will happen to Vavi, or her baby, when they most certainly kill Gorren.

I try to untangle it all, to come up with the right solution, but it feels hopeless. I wish we'd never come here. I wish I'd never seen Jar'kel outside of city council.

Eventually I fall asleep, wishing I were back home in my own bed.

CHAPTER 7

JAR'KEL

Perhaps I should be kinder to her. Simka is young, after all, and doesn't have the same capacity to contain her emotions as I do. But I hate hearing her cry, because it doesn't fit her character. She's stronger than this—or so I thought.

Instead, I've been disappointed by someone again.

When Pa'zi told me she was leaving me, there were no tears. I wasn't surprised. A few weeks later, she departed Attirex with her new lover, and then I knew the truth: I'd been second for a long time, and she was simply waiting for the right moment to tell me.

That's always how these things end. Disappointment.

Eventually Simka quiets. At least she'll have some rest after all this. Perhaps I should've stayed in the bed so she would have a warm body next to hers. I know how comforting it can be to simply not sleep alone.

But that would be foolish. My body would undoubtedly react to hers so close, after the way it betrayed me on our journey. It's best that we stay apart.

At last, when the fire has burned down to embers, I drift away into darkness.

Unfortunately, we're awakened too soon by the sound of the tent flap opening, and an orc arrives carrying our breakfast. He freezes in the doorway as I sit up in my bed on the floor.

"Lover's quarrel?" he asks with a sly grin as he sets the tray down and retrieves the one from last night. Simka and I must have some special standing here, with her being the sister of the clan leader's mate, or we wouldn't be served like royalty this way.

"If that's what you want to call it," I say, leaving my furs on the ground. The fresh cut of meat is more than appetizing after the slim rations we had on the way up.

Simka is still dead asleep, and not even our voices have stirred her.

"You should go," I tell him. "Let her have her rest."

After the orc's gone, I make sure only to eat half of what we were given. Eventually Simka does awaken, and she's bleary-eyed with a puffy face. She must have cried for a long time. I didn't expect it from someone as tough as she is.

She crawls out of bed long enough to retrieve the tray, then scurries back to the furs with it. She doesn't speak at all, and when she's finished, she drops the tray on the floor and lies back down.

"Pouting isn't going to help," I tell her as I get to my feet. I plan on exploring the camp today and getting a lay of the land. I need to be prepared for the moment when Gorren and his forces are away and I can slip out, unseen.

"I'm not pouting." Simka finally looks at me with her lips squeezed tight together, her brow furrowed.

"Looks like a pout to me." I stretch my arms, then my legs, and head for the door.

"Where are you going?" I don't miss the tiny tinge of fear in her voice, like my leaving her alone might expose her to some kind of danger.

"Out." I leave quickly, so I don't have to look at her any longer. The urge to sit down on the bed and comfort her was powerful, but that won't help anything. She needs to be tough to get through whatever is coming, and strength doesn't come from pampering.

Outside, the camp is alive with activity. I'd been under the impression that like wild trolls, wild orcs were uncivilized, disorganized, and mad with their bloodlust. Instead, they're carrying wood, carcasses, and leather working supplies from one place to another all across the camp, each with their own important tasks. A few whelps are playing a game nearby, trying to toss bones past a stick planted in the snow. I even spot a human here and there, men and women alike, doing their share of the work.

I stroll about the camp, attracting far too much attention as the singular troll among the lot of them. But this is good. They'll get accustomed to my presence soon, and then when I make my move, no one will look twice at me.

Suddenly, someone slaps me on the back, and I whirl around. My hand goes to the hilt of my sword. The wild orcs didn't take it from me, which shows a surprising amount of trust based on very little besides Simka's word that we are, in fact, mates.

"Whoa there," Gorren says, holding up both arms in surrender. "Just wishing you a good morning."

I let out a breath and release my sword. "Thanks." I try my hardest to appear relaxed.

"Sleep well?" He winks, and I'm taken aback at how this gruff orc seems to have a playful side.

"Well enough." I nod. "Thank you for the food."

He chuckles. "No need to thank me. I want Vavi's young sister to feel comfortable and happy here." The amusement fades from his face. "Can't have her wanting to leave, can I?"

"Of course. She wouldn't want to leave her beloved sister." I try to smile in return. "Or such a luxurious fur bed."

A booming laugh comes out of him. "Good. I expect you'll have some whelps of your own soon." He cocks his head. "You don't have much time, troll, so you'd better get busy."

I recognize the dig at my age for what it is. "My parents were older when they had me, and I turned out fine." A partial truth. I was still a whelp myself when they passed away, and my only brother had long moved on. Most of my young adulthood was spent fending for myself.

"Good." Gorren gestures at the open space, where a big pit has been dug in the snow and a structure of logs assembled in it. "Tonight we will have a celebration for the two of you and your matehood." Gorren glances around us, looking for something. He spots whatever it is a few tents away and calls out, "Vavi!"

Quickly, Vavi bounces over to us, looking ripe and full to bursting with whelp. He pulls her into his arms and his hands skim eagerly over her body, as if I'm not even standing here. "You never got a proper mating ceremony, I imagine, living among the Herded?" Gorren asks in Trollkin.

"Herded?" I ask, genuinely not sure what he means.

"The others." His eyebrows lower, and his voice turns dangerous. "The fools who have decided to tie themselves to kings and chieftains." He pats me on the shoulder, and his face softens. "But no more of that for you. Your bond will be celebrated here." He kisses Vavi, and she returns it. "We expect a good show tonight."

"A... show?" I ask, dreading what that might entail.

"The strength of your bond shining bright," Gorren answers.

Vavi glances between us as we speak in Trollkin, then frowns at Gorren. "You know I don't like it when I can't understand you," she grumps.

He just grins at her, kissing away her pout. "Sorry."

Before they walk away, Vavi turns to me. "We look forward to the party, corporal," she says with a wink.

Great. This is the worst news I've gotten since I was sent to this horrid place.

SIMKA

Jar'kel's right. I am pouting.

Really, I'm mourning. As much as I want to believe we can find a way out of here, I also know it won't be that easy, not with how heavily this place is guarded. I would have thought Vavi might try to help me, but now I highly doubt it. It's like a spell has been cast over her.

I barely recognize my sister.

More than an hour has passed and I'm still sitting on the bed, holding the empty tray when the tent flap opens. I'm about to say something nasty to Jar'kel, but it's Vavi stepping inside, instead.

"Simka!" She runs over and seats herself next to me. I still can't fathom how that rather large swell in her belly came to be.

While she's been getting fat and happy here, we thought of nothing but her. It infuriates me.

"How was it?" Vavi asks, eyebrow raised mischievously.

I give her a blank look. "How was what?"

"Having your own tent." She's practically vibrating with excitement. "I can't imagine you and Jar'kel have had an easy journey so far. Life on the outside isn't very open to human-trollkin relationships. I'm sure Dad didn't approve."

Internally, I cringe. It feels wrong lying to my own sister, but in a way, I feel like she lied to me, too. She let us believe she was dead, or worse—all because she fell head-over-heels for some *orc*.

"It was lovely," I answer carefully. "Just like you said, Dad wasn't too happy, so we had to keep it secret."

Vavi squints, though, like she doesn't believe me. "Then why did I hear that Jar'kel slept on the floor?"

Fuck. That's all going to have to be a part of this ruse, isn't it? My stomach twists into a knot. Jar'kel would probably rather die than share the bed with me, but that could very well be the choice we face.

I wave her away casually. "I toss and turn in my sleep. I think he got tired of me kicking him."

For once, her face is unreadable. Does she suspect that I'm hiding something?

"That's odd," Vavi says. "No one heard you last night."

"Huh?" I squint in confusion. "Heard what?"

"You know." She elbows me in the side. "Doing the dirty."

Double fuck. Jar'kel and I, doing *that*? I can't fathom it, but at the same time... An image pops into my head of the two of us in the fur bed together, him naked and on top of me, and my entire body turns blistering hot.

"Oh," I manage, trying to come up with a good excuse while my face burns. "Well, uh, we were tired. I fell asleep before we could..." I wave my hands. "You know. Do anything."

Vavi narrows her eyes. "Simka." I swallow at the sound of her "mom" voice. She used it from time to time when we were growing up, only when it was something was serious.

"Yes?" I ask meekly.

"You two have had sex already, right?" She narrows her eyes. "You're not a virgin anymore?"

I'm a terrible liar, and my sister has always seen right through me. But if I tell her the truth, she'll know that Jar'kel and I have been fleecing her. So I put on my best cool face, trying to channel his stony voice, and say, "I'm not."

After studying me for a moment, Vavi lets out a relieved sigh.

"Good. Because as soon as the mating bond sets in, there's no way around it." Her eyes glitter. "Gorren and I have been at it like rabbits since, well... since I realized."

Right.

"We've been doing the same thing," I say, mustering as much confidence as I can. "Can't get enough of each other."

Vavi grins. "Well, you don't need to keep it a secret anymore. They're very open here about sex. *Very* open. Be as loud as you want."

"Oh." Immediately I think about what kinds of sounds I might make if Jar'kel were wrapped around me—or inside me. It's both strange and horribly erotic. "Thanks for letting me know," I squeak out.

"Of course." Vavi takes both of my hands in hers and smiles brightly. "I want my only sister to be happy here, like I am."

I furrow my brow at how genuinely pleased she sounds. How can she be so cavalier about all of this while our village mourns those who were taken? While Dad and I mourned *her*?

"You know that Dad thinks you're dead, right?" I finally say, and I can't disguise the irritation in my voice. "While you're snuggling with some orc, Dad is back home and all alone."

Her happy face falls, and I break our contact. "Yeah," she says in an uncertain voice. "I try not to think about it. There's nothing I can do, Simka. I can't leave here, either."

I stare at her. "You're a prisoner? And you haven't tried to escape?"

Vavi just furrows her brow. "I'm not a prisoner. I *want* to be here. I want to be with Gorren, and raise our baby together."

Do we really mean so little to her? Less than some guy she's known for six months?

"You could at least have told us," I finally say, my tone guarded. "You should've found a way to send us a message, so we would know you were all right."

"There's no way I could get a message to Dad without revealing everything!" Vavi stands up, wringing her hands together. "I'm sorry, Simka, but I'm... I'm here for a reason. And that reason is very important."

I peer at her. "What reason is that, Vavi?"

She bites her lip, then looks away. I know whatever she's about to say is a half-truth. "I'm protecting the clan. I believe in what Gorren believes in."

"Which is what?" I demand. "Attacking the mine? Stealing people like you from their homes in the middle of the night?"

Vavi's shoulders curl tightly around her neck, like she's protecting herself from my barbs. "I know it looks that way," she says, keeping her gaze on the floor. "But there are a lot of things you don't understand yet, Simka."

"Then explain them to me!" I'm breathing hard, furious that she won't tell me the truth. "Tell me why you won't even *try* to go back home."

"Because I can be with Gorren here. Because I have a purpose here." She bunches her hands up into fists. "And it's an important one."

I just want to shake her. "And what sort of 'purpose' is so important that you couldn't try to return to your *family*?" I pour venom into the word, and she flinches.

Holding her shoulders up around her neck, she begins. "The night the orcs took me," Vavi says, "I wasn't afraid."

Chapter 8

Simka

How could she not have been afraid? That's impossible. The wild orcs had appeared out of nowhere, coming down the mountain and spreading across the village like a plague.

But it's true that Vavi hadn't screamed when they barged into the house. She hadn't fought. Could she really have known then?

"Then why?" I finally ask. "Why did you lock me in the cellar if you were so sure they wouldn't hurt you?"

She looks down at the floor. "Because I didn't want you to have to watch them take me away."

"But Vavi, they're..." I search for the right word. "They're monsters. You couldn't have known!"

"I don't know how else to explain it. I just understood that they weren't going to hurt me."

My sister's always been a bit of the fanciful sort, but this is surprising even for her.

"Simka." Vavi looks deep into my eyes, and I return the look firmly. "I know it seems strange to you now. But I was led here for a reason. A very important reason." She pushes a stray lock of my short hair away from my face. "I am a guardian. I was brought to Gorren so that he could be one, too."

"A guardian?" I ask cautiously. "Of what?"

"Of the secrets these mountains hold," she says. "The clan came here to protect those secrets. That's why they siege the Grand Chieftain's mine. They're trying to keep him away from the power underneath the stone."

I stare at her. "What are you talking about?" It sounds like she's truly lost her mind. "What kind of power?"

"Something far greater than you can imagine. Something ancient and..." Vavi trails off, looking thoughtful. "It doesn't matter. I'm here so that together, Gorren and I can save the world."

My mouth falls open. Vavi never had delusions of grandeur before. Something has changed in the time we were apart, and now she's lost her mind.

"And you're here for the same reason, Simka." Vavi's happy, carefree demeanor fades, and she's serious as she regards me. "Jar'kel, too. I know you hate being away from Dad, but right now, this is where you're needed. To help protect the mountains' secret. To keep power out of the wrong hands." She sighs sadly. "I wish there was some way we could tell him where we are, that we're safe, but there just isn't. I hope you can understand."

No, I don't understand a lick more than I did before, except now I'm sure that my sister's crazy.

"What is this all-important secret?" I ask, my voice rising as my anger gets the better of me. "I want to know what you gave us up for. What was so important that you let us grieve you."

She looks into my eyes for a long time, so long that I start to wonder if she heard me. But then, Vavi stands up. "I'm sorry, Simka. You're not ready yet."

I get to my feet, too, glaring at her, and gesture to the door. "Fine. When you finally trust me enough—your own *sister*—to tell me the truth, let me know."

Vavi studies me, her eyes darting to my hands, which shake in my anger. With a nod of understanding she departs the tent, letting the flap fall closed behind her.

I'd hoped and begged to see my sister again, but not like this. I miss things the way they were at home, when we both lived in Dad's house and I understood everything about her. She was my best friend then, but now it feels like she's a different person—a stranger, almost. A stranger who thinks she was sent here for some mysterious reason that was more important than her own family.

I fall back to the bed, covering my face. Only moments later, Jar'kel steps inside. I rub my cheeks, hoping the heat of our argument will dissipate, but the intense look he gives me doesn't help. His eyes are stern and set.

"Jar'kel," I say, at the same moment he says, "Simka. We have to talk."

I balk at his tone. "About what?"

"About what they expect from us here." He approaches where I'm sitting, and I realize then just how tall he is. His shoulders are broad, exceptionally so, and his uniform only emphasizes the point.

That image pops into my head again, of his sweating body on top of mine, and even my ears feel like they're on fire.

"That's what I need to talk about with you, too." I stare down at my feet as I speak. "We have to sleep in the bed together. Word has already gotten around that you were on the floor last night. And apparently, um, mates don't do that."

The ghost of a smile pulls up Jar'kel's lip. "Indeed. Mates fuck. A lot."

I bury my face in my hands at his word choice. "How can you be so crass?"

"It's a crass thing, isn't it?"

"I wouldn't know," I say, in my quietest voice possible.

He cocks his head, lowering his ear towards me. "What's that?"

"Nothing!" I sit up straight. "So we have to sleep in the same bed. What were you going to tell me?" Maybe it won't be so bad. We could keep each other warm, at least, which I wouldn't mind.

"That's not all we have to do." This time, it's Jar'kel who lets out the bone-deep sigh. "At the celebration tonight. They expect us to *act* like mates, too."

My stomach falls. "What does that mean?"

He shoots me a look like I'm an idiot. "What do you think? You saw the way Gorren was all over your sister."

Oh. Like that.

"So you have to put your hands on me." The disgusted look on his face when I say it makes my heart twist. He really hates the idea of it that much? I do my best to scowl back at him, because if he thinks I'm below him, then he's below me, too. "It's just for now, though. And then we're out of here, right?"

Jar'kel folds up the blankets he slept on last night and returns them to the bed. "Yes. I'm looking for a way out every moment. Distractions are the best way to overcome a disadvantage— whether we find one, or come up with one ourselves."

"As long as Vavi doesn't get hurt." I narrow my eyes. "When the city guard storms the camp, you'll make sure she's safe, right?"

Jar'kel watches me silently, and I can't tell what he's thinking under there. Eventually, though, he nods in assent.

"I'll make sure of it. And we'll do what we have to do to get by until then."

I square my shoulders. "At the celebration tonight, we'll put on the best act possible."

"That we will."

I consider telling him about my conversation with Vavi, about this "secret" that lives inside the mountain, but surely Jar'kel wouldn't believe it, either. He would just think me a silly girl believing silly fairy tales.

So I keep it to myself for now, wondering what my sister knows that I don't.

JAR'KEL

When night falls, the bonfire is lit, and the celebration begins. Big barrels of mead are rolled out and opened, and I make sure to take a mug and hold it, occasionally pretending to take a sip. I need to stay alert and observe, to get a sense of the organization of the camp and where the orcs' weak spots lie. It will be more difficult, of course, worrying about how I'll get Simka out along with me. But at least she's capable and strong, quick and quiet.

I couldn't imagine leaving her behind anyway. She may not like me much, but we got into this mess together, and I intend to get us out of it together, too. She saved my life. I owe her that much.

Side by side we settle at one of the tables erected around the fire, to the left of Gorren and Vavi. A boar has been cooking since the early morning, and the clan leader is the first to cut into it, offering the choicest innards to his mate. Vavi reluctantly takes it, and it appears that in some ways, she hasn't become fully accustomed to the clan's culture. That's good. When the city guard takes the camp and inevitably kills Gorren, she and her whelp will live, and someday, she'll move on. Though trollkin rarely survive a mate's death, I doubt the bond affects humans.

When the festivities begin and Gorren toasts to us, I wrap an arm around Simka's waist, as instructed. At first she's stiff and hard against me, but as she drinks the mead and the night grows colder, she scoots closer. Every place I'm touching her, my skin feels too hot, and I have to remove the little cloak she gave me to let some of the heat out.

Vavi wanders over to us, settling her hand on her sister's shoulder. "You're so stiff, *corporal*," Vavi says. "You can let loose a little, you know."

Simka bristles. "That's just how he is. We had to keep this secret for so long, you know."

"Oh, of course." Vavi lets it drop, and moves on again to greet the other orcs. But Gorren has been staring at me for some time, and while I can't make out his expression, I don't like it.

I lean down to whisper to Simka. "You should sit in my lap."

She glares up at me. "What?"

"So they believe us. Here." I pat my leg, and Simka stares at it with disbelief. But then, after an irritated shake of her head, she crawls into my lap, seating herself on my thighs.

Instantaneously, the sensation of her butt on my crotch lights me up like a torch. I don't know how long it's been since I touched anyone this way, and my cock is very aware. When the soft curve of her ass brushes over it, I have to bite my tongue to keep myself under control.

"Like this?" Simka asks uneasily, trying to find a comfortable spot. I slide an arm around her waist to keep her secured.

"Now don't move," I say, because if she rubs that pert ass of hers over me again, my infernal body might just be forced to respond.

She goes stiff. "I'll, uh, try."

Simka clutches her mug tight against her chest, and she takes my instruction very seriously, with even her breath coming in short, controlled bursts. I roll my eyes.

"You don't have to turn into wood," I tell her. "That's not going to help our case."

"I don't know what you want me to do." Her voice goes quiet. "I'm sorry."

I sigh, and instinctively rub her back. "Relax. Try to imagine I'm someone else. Someone you like, maybe."

If anything, she gets even more rigid. I wonder who else she's thinking of?

Jealousy sparks at this thought. But no, she had a life before this. Maybe there's someone she fancied back in her village.

I grit my teeth and try not to think of who else might have touched Simka this way.

It feels like hours pass with neither of us speaking, simply picking at our shared plate of roasted tubers and seared elk, and drinking the orcs' odd-tasting mead. After a time, I chance a look at Gorren and Vavi, who are settled in together with his arm loosely around her middle, his hand gliding over her full breasts. She giggles and leans into him as he tweaks her nipple under her tunic, and his other hand dives down between her legs.

They aren't the only ones. As the night has gone on and more mead has disappeared, the other orcs are growing bolder, dancing in front of the flames, grinding their bodies against one another. I can't help but be mesmerized by their silhouettes as they fondle and hold each other close. There's another big, male orc and a human woman, and she's dressed the same as any of the other wild orcs. She's fully integrated, it looks like, by the way he's holding her with her legs wrapped around his waist and kissing her.

I wonder what it would be like to touch Simka that way. To dance in front of the fire. To bring her warm body against mine, and feel every inch of her under my hands.

When I look up, I find Gorren observing me again.

"You're so stiff, corporal," he says in Trollkin. "You can be yourself here, you know. There's no one here to judge you. Claim your mate. Have fun." He narrows his eyes. "She's your mate."

Fuck. We're still not being very convincing. But if I don't keep up the ruse, he could decide to kill me, and who knows what would become of Simka? He needs to think we're telling the truth, until he lets his guard down.

I breathe in through my nose, then boldly circle Simka with my arms. She shoots me a questioning look over her shoulder as I cradle her body tightly against mine.

"You're the one who sold this to Gorren and Vavi," I whisper to her, splaying my four-fingered hand over her belly to keep her anchored to me. She shifts on my lap, and I almost groan as her ass brushes over my cock.

"I did it to keep you alive," she hisses back.

"You're not being a very good saleswoman from where I'm sitting." I don't know why I'm taunting her. I shouldn't want this. Pretending to be bound to Simka ought to feel like a chore.

Instead, my hands wander up over her body, pausing under the swell of her breasts. The shape of them is hard to make out under her thick clothes, but I know they would be soft and round. My cock leaps under my pants, and I squeeze my eyes shut, willing it to calm down.

This is a natural reaction. Any warm body on top of mine would elicit this response.

But even I know that's a lie.

CHAPTER 9

SIMKA

I try to hold in my gasp as Jar'kel's hand slides up my side, pausing at my ribcage before brushing over my chest. Instantly my nipples harden into tiny rocks, and when he passes over them again, I can't help squirming. It feels far too good.

"Simka," Jar'kel chides quietly. I bite my lip, trying to stay still as he runs his hand back over my hardened nipple, then down my belly. "If you keep moving like that..." He doesn't finish his sentence, but I think I can figure it out. If he's anything like a human man, he has a cock there between his legs.

"I'm trying not to move," I whimper. I hate how pathetic I sound, but I'm torn between wanting him to stop and wanting him to keep going. How can he be so nonchalant about this? I'm leaning into his touch, and the empty place at the crux of my thighs is struggling to find friction. I shouldn't want this grouchy old troll's hands all over me, and yet a tingle is trickling down into my belly and spreading to my arms and legs. I feel myself clench-ing, opening and closing for something that isn't there.

"Please," I whimper as his fingers graze over my pelvis. I can't possibly stay still while he touches me this way, when all my body wants is to respond to his. And here? In front of everyone? "Please don't."

Jar'kel stops very abruptly, and his body becomes hard as rock under mine. I can barely hear his muttered "sorry" as he slides me off his lap and gets to his feet. With a tight expression, he picks up his mug. "More mead," he grunts, and strides away without a look back.

But instead of stopping at the barrels of mead, he keeps going and disappears into the camp.

I sit there, stunned, for far too long. Then I glance around to determine if anyone saw me being spurned by my supposed-mate, but the rest of the orcs are consumed in their own activities. That's when I notice that Vavi's tunic is pulled up over her belly, and her pants are around her knees. As horrifying as it is, I can't tear my gaze away from what I see: Gorren's thick, green cock is sliding into her, then out again, soaked in her wetness. She cries out, and his hands cup her belly tightly as he fucks her at the table right next to us.

They aren't the only ones. Around the flames I spot another couple, a male orc and a male human, both of them grunting and groaning as the orc sinks himself deep into his human mate. My whole body lights on fire, from my face to my toes, and a ball of pure lightning strikes me right at the base of my hips.

What's happening here? It's like some mad spell has fallen over the camp. I clamp my legs together tight, hoping Jar'kel will come back. But the sounds of lovemaking only grow louder as time wears on, and still, I'm alone.

He's abandoned me.

I've seen sex before, but it was never so... in my face. Once, when I was out feeding Fio late at night, I discovered Vavi and one of the village boys locked at the hips behind the shed. I screeched and covered Fio's eyes, but it was dark, and I didn't see much myself. But I still knew what they were doing.

Later, Vavi told me everything—how sex had felt somewhat unpleasant the first time, but she'd still enjoyed it. *And each time it gets better*, she'd said. After that I made sure she was drinking purentea, and told her I never wanted to see her behind the shed again.

Now here she is, doing it right in the middle of a crowd. I don't even recognize the woman who once snuck off into a dark corner to do the deed.

Surrounded by groaning orcs, all of them reveling in their bodies, I think of sitting on Jar'kel's lap, where I could feel... *him*, through his pants. Just the idea of what's underneath makes heat lance through my body and pool at the base of my hips.

What's happening? Something about this place has infected me. I have to get away before it burrows any deeper into me.

I leap off the bench and sprint through the camp, heading straight for our tent. When I rip the flap aside, I find Jar'kel there, sitting on the bed with his head in his hands. He looks up when I enter, and his expression is... strangely vulnerable. Open to me, showing me just a glimmer of the real troll hiding underneath that hardened face.

I don't want him to see how the gathering at the bonfire affected me, so I dive for the bed, burying myself as deep under the furs as possible. I can't get images of the orcs out of my mind, their bodies gyrating, their cocks glistening with fluid. I don't notice that I'm shaking all over until a hand brushes my arm, and I still myself. The last thing I want is to act sensitive where Jar'kel can see me—but I have nowhere else to hide.

"Get away from me," I say, but my voice cracks in the middle. His hand stops moving, but doesn't leave me.

"What happened?" he asks. Even though I can't see his face from inside my cocoon, I can picture his condescending expression.

"Them," is all I can answer. "All of them. Even Vavi, doing that, right there in front of everyone." I clench my hands into fists and grit my teeth. "*Fucking.*"

Using that crude word lights my body up again, and I groan into the pillow.

"It was too much for you, wasn't it?" Jar'kel asks, more quietly than I've ever heard him.

"No, it wasn't," I say, even though it's a filthy lie. Everything is too much, and I don't know what to do with all of this raw need rising up inside me. I want him to touch me, even now, and it's terrifying. I've never craved hands on me like this, and there's nothing else more awful.

But the way he reacted, like I was disgusting, is a spear buried in my chest. And then to see all of the orcs out there, doing *that...*

I have to get out of here.

Jar'kel says nothing, but he starts stroking my hair in soothing, steady motion. I wonder what it means. Does he pity me? Is this sympathy?

But he doesn't move or speak. After my lungs have calmed, I feel nothing but exhausted, and it's easy to slide into sleep.

JAR'KEL

Poor Simka.

She is tough and strong for her age. She can fight, but that doesn't mean the world can't touch her. She's been thrust into the middle of something strange and supremely foreign. I wish for a moment that I could help, that I could impart some kind of wisdom to make this easier for her. Much to my discredit, our act affected me, too. I couldn't look away from what was happening out there, the intimacy on bare display. I had to leave her. I couldn't trust myself, and rarely—if ever—have I lost control. But her body was too pliable, too warm, too perfectly curved and swelled in all the right places that I almost lost myself in it.

But she clearly doesn't want that from me, not this innocent woman. The moment she told me to stop, reality came rushing back, and I couldn't stand it for a moment longer.

So now I stay at her side, the steady presence she clearly craves. Eventually her shivering stops, and her breathing settles. When I'm certain she's fallen asleep, I get under the furs, keeping one of them balled up between us. Maybe we have to share this bed, but I don't want to make her even more uncomfortable than she already is—even though I want nothing more than to wrap her up, to bring her in close, to keep her safe from everything outside this tent that wants to hurt her.

Simka rolls over in her sleep, searching for something with her hands. She curls them around the fur and pulls it in close, crushing it against her body as she sleeps. If that were me instead...

I'm getting soft towards this girl, and that's the opposite of what needs to happen. Of course I will try my best to get her out when the time comes to leave. She should be back in her home, in her bed, in her old life.

But that's all. We will go our separate ways once our mission is finished, her to her village and me to my desert. I'll finally be released from the Grand Chieftain's orders, and my life can resume as normal.

I will do that one thing, I decide. I will make sure we both emerge from this safely, and then my debt to her for saving my life will be paid in full.

CHAPTER 10

SIMKA

I awaken to a gentle creaking sound.

Wait. It's not a door hinge, but something else, something throatier. When I peer out from under the furs, Jar'kel is passed out beside me, snoring.

I've never thought that someone's snores could be appealing, almost sweet. For once his face is relaxed, his brows loose, his mouth no longer curled down in a scowl. He has far fewer wrinkles like this, and he appears ten years younger. I find myself reaching out to push some of his hair away from his face, but stop myself just before touching him. It would be a shame if he woke up now.

I like seeing him this way.

So I watch him, listening as the camp wakes up and orcs start moving about outside our tent. It isn't until someone slides a breakfast tray into our tent that Jar'kel's eyes fly open, and his pupils shrink to tiny points as he registers me.

"Simka." The word falls from his lips in a breath, but he doesn't move away like I expected. No, his red-orange eyes peer steadily into mine. I don't even breathe, waiting for the moment he jumps from the bed to get on with his day, probably with some sharp retort.

"Good morning." It's the only thing I can think of to say. Of course I can't tell him how comforting it was to sleep next to him, how happy and safe I felt waking up to his face.

Eventually he sighs, brow furrowing again like it always does. His typical irritation returns. "Do you feel all right?"

I squeeze the furs in my hands to keep them from reaching out to touch him. That's all I want, to smooth my hands over the crinkled planes of his face and convince him to let his guard down.

"Yes." Ever so slightly, I curl towards him. "I feel fine."

His chest falls as he expels a breath. "Good. I... was worried about you last night."

He was worried about me? I didn't think he worried about anyone.

"I wouldn't have guessed that by the way you left," I say.

Jar'kel cringes.

"I guess you weren't doing so well, either," I amend. "It was a strange evening."

"Yes, it was."

We lie there, looking at each other for what feels like much too long, but also not long enough. I could stare into his eyes for an eternity, I think. There's so much to see there, so many old injuries and disappointments to unravel.

"We should eat," Jar'kel says, breaking the silence. When he sits up, he's only wearing his undershirt, his coat hanging off a wood rack in the corner of the tent. I like how the tight shirt fits his bare body. I wonder what his chest would feel like under my hands if he touched me of his own volition, rather than as part of our ruse. If he touched me because he wanted to.

Jar'kel pads over to the food, and when I don't leave the bed, he brings it back and sets it down next to me, dividing it into two portions.

While we're eating, though, someone taps on the post holding up the tent flap. "What is it?" I call out, wondering if they're already here to collect our tray. The flap flies open and Vavi barges inside.

"Oh." She pauses, seeing that the two of us are still in bed. A wide smile spreads across her face. "Should I leave you?"

I want to say *yes*, but I can sense our window of unguarded time has closed. Jar'kel tenses up again, and I hurry off the bed to greet her.

"Come for a walk with me?" she asks, offering me her arm. I turn back to Jar'kel, but he's already waving me away dismissively as he cleans up.

"Sure," I say, wishing he'd given me a reason not to go.

We start off, Vavi leading us to the edge of the camp, where a path leads up into the mountains. We hike for a while in silence, until we stop abruptly at a pile of big rocks. There she gestures for me to sit.

"I didn't hear anything coming from your tent last night," she observes, arching an eyebrow.

Fuck. I forgot about that. What right does she have, anyway, to give a rat's ass about my sex life?

"Jar'kel isn't the loud type," I say defensively. "And we were tired after all the partying."

"Again?" Suspicion settles over her face. "You're not lying to me, are you?"

I blanch. "Why would I lie to my own sister?" My feigned outrage is partially real. She's the one keeping me prisoner here, forcing me into this stupid arrangement. I *am* angry with her.

"I don't know." Vavi runs a hand down her belly. "I just thought it would be nice for our kids to play together. To grow up together."

She doesn't seem to understand that there's a countdown, a time limit, to whatever it is the orcs are doing here. I'm not the world's best tracker—just the most determined one. Anyone more skilled will find them here eventually if they keep up their attacks on the mine.

"I want our kids to grow up together, too," I say, and take her hand in mine. "Jar'kel and I are just not certain that's what we want yet." It feels plausible enough.

"Really?" Her eyebrows raise. "But the mating bond. As soon as they feel it, you know, that's all they can think about. Popping out kids. Gorren wouldn't stop fucking me until he was sure he'd succeeded." She laughs. "Actually, he still hasn't stopped."

I shrug. "I guess Jar'kel is different."

Rubbing her chin, she nods. "I'm not surprised. He's older. But that means you should start sooner rather than later."

I don't like her implication that there's a time limit—that Jar'kel is bound by how long he has left.

"Right," I say. I'm getting cold, so I stand up and wrap my arms around myself. "Can we go back now?"

Vavi studies me like she's trying to make sense of me. We always understood each other before, but now it feels as if there's a gaping chasm between us.

"Sure." She gets up and takes my hand, the way she did when we were girls. "Let's go back so you can be with your troll again."

JAR'KEL

There's not much to do with myself here. We're served our meals, and as guests of the clan leader, apparently aren't expected to pull our own weight. I don't like being idle, but I have one job here, and it's to find a way out.

LYONNE RILEY

When Simka returns from her walk with her sister, she has a look in her eye I can't identify. She sits down in front of the fire and I join her a few feet away.

"We have to do a better job of faking it," she says eventually, not looking at me. "My sister doesn't believe us."

Wonderful. As if it hasn't been uncomfortable enough already. "What else can we do?" I put another log on the fire and stir it.

Simka hesitates. "She, um, doesn't understand why we don't want babies."

Oh. I suppose that makes sense. I've seen it myself, the way that the mating bond takes over, how it settles deep inside a trollkin and drives them toward one singular purpose. Last I saw, my former captain and her lieutenant had two whelps with a third one on the way. I imagine they have quite an active private life.

"I see." This can only mean one thing, and I don't like it. "Then we had better do a better job of pretending."

Simka nods uneasily. I know how my hands on her had disturbed her, and I don't want to have to do it again. Not unless it's real, and it never will be. She's young and has a whole life ahead of her, and she'd never want an old fuck like me.

"Did you ask when the orcs are planning their next attack?" I ask, trying to change the subject. "Your sister likely knows."

Simka's shoulders curl up, and a guilty look flashes across her face.

I tilt my head. "What is it?" She's not so great at hiding what she feels.

"Vavi wouldn't tell me something like that," Simka says in a low whisper. "There's no way."

I narrow my eyes. "Why not? She must trust you. You're her sister."

Simka just shakes her head. "No. She's already suspicious of me, and that would make it worse." She tenses even further.

74

"There's something strange going on here, Jar'kel. More than just orcs having orgies at the bonfire."

I have to chuckle. It's good she still has her sense of humor. "Strange in what way?" I ask.

Simka hesitates, like she's not sure how much she should share with me—which piques my interest even more. Her lip screws up, and her eyes dart everywhere in the tent that isn't my face.

Finally, though, it seems she's decided to let out whatever she's bottling up inside.

"Vavi thinks she's some kind of *guardian,*" Simka says, even quieter. She picks at the fur on the edge of her cloak, something I've noticed is a habit of hers when she feels uneasy. "She believes she was sent here for a purpose. And that I'm here for the same reason."

"A purpose? Besides popping out whelps for the clan leader?"

Simka explains to me about the power underneath the mountain, how her sister believes they were both destined to help protect it. "The Blue Crags are special," she says. "Even I know that. But not because of some hidden power."

Is this why the wild orcs appeared when they did? To keep safe whatever it is they believe is underneath the mountains?

If Simka can't get any more information out of her sister, then it's up to me to befriend Gorren and learn the answers myself.

Rising to my feet, I dust off my pants. I know what I need to do. Perhaps if I can understand why the orcs are here, what this power is that they seek to protect, it could help me formulate my escape plan.

"Where are you going?" Simka asks.

"To get some answers." Perhaps if I make myself invaluable—and worthy of his trust—Gorren will tell me what I want to know.

CHAPTER 11

JAR'KEL

Gorren is in the leader's tent, a great big structure of hide stretched among a number of thick log poles. The door is held open with a leather tie, so I peek my head in, hoping he won't be offended at my unannounced arrival.

"Corporal!" Gorren's booming voice takes me by surprise. He approaches me with three long strides and slaps me heavily on the shoulder. "I'm glad you finally stopped by. I didn't want to interrupt you and your mate, but I'm in need of your assistance."

I blink. "Mine?"

"Of course!" He leads me into the tent, where two other orcs are gathered around a big map, drawn on leather. "You know so much that would be useful to us."

I have to be careful about what I reveal to him. Putting the city guard in danger is out of the question, but I need to give him just enough to make me a part of his plans.

"I'm not sure what I can offer," I hedge.

But Gorren just grins. "Don't play coy. As one of the former city guard, you're a valuable asset." He taps on the map. "We are looking for train schedules, guard rotations, anything you know that would be helpful in coordinating an attack."

Shit. I do know the answer to a lot of his questions, because I came on one of those trains myself from my barren desert, and the guard rotation is burned into my memory. I worked night shifts, and dreaded every time the sun went down.

Gorren surveys me as I hesitate, his thick eyebrows lowering. "Perhaps you need some persuasion."

That doesn't sound good. What is this orc willing to do to get what he wants?

Gorren laughs at my expression. "Whatever you're thinking, it's not that." He stoops down and fishes around for something under the table. The other two orcs in the room stand up and back away, and I wonder if I should, too.

At last, Gorren brings something out. It's a clay jar, which he sets down on top of the map.

"Come on, corporal," he urges. "Come look."

When he opens the lid, radiant purple light seeps out of the gaps, as if starlight has been trapped inside it. He sets the lid aside, revealing the pot is full of some sort of glowing liquid. I'm so astonished that I say the first thing that comes to mind.

"What the hell is that?"

Gorren chuckles and swishes the pot, causing the mixture inside to slosh about. The other two orcs tense as if he has a stick of dynamite in his hand. "Magic."

The word doesn't make sense to me. Sometimes magic features in children's stories, where once upon a time, trollkin like us could wield it, until the world changed and moved on. Now it's a figment of our imaginations, a power beyond what the mortal realm can handle.

I laugh. I can't help it. It comes out of me in a burst, and Gorren frowns.

"Sorry," I say, rubbing my stump of a tusk. "It's just ridiculous. *Magic.*"

With a stern face, Gorren sets the pot on the table. "This is quite serious, corporal. This is why we left our own true home deeper in the mountains and came here. And it's the reason you should help us."

Instead of replying, I wait for him to explain himself.

"Everything we do is for the preservation of magic," he continues, "and to prevent those who shouldn't have it from getting their hands on it."

He dips one hand into the pot, and comes out with a few droplets of the purple liquid sticking to his finger. Holding it up, he closes his eyes and speaks: "Give me gold."

I chuckle. "Sorry, I don't have any."

But Gorren shakes his head. I wait and watch as the liquid... changes. He rolls it down into his palm and there, it hardens into a ball of what is certainly gold.

I simply stand there, staring, unsure of what I've just seen. He juggles it from one hand to the other, then offers it to me. I take the tiny nugget and examine it, tapping one side with my fingernail.

"Real gold," I mutter. This can't be right. No, it's wrong—very wrong. I hand the gold back to him as if it's dirty.

Gorren chuckles as he takes the nugget back. "You see the danger?" he says, dropping it on the table. "Anything you want, it will become that. Anything you wish, it will happen. In the wrong hands, it could do incredible damage." He tucks his arms behind his back and returns to the map, ushering me over to look.

I still don't believe it's real, despite just seeing it with my own eyes.

"Here," he says, tapping a familiar spot on the parchment. His finger is near Morgenzan, inside the mountain.

I nod. "The mine."

"It's not the mine that's important to me." He crouches down to return the pot to its hidden place under the table. "I care about what's underneath. Magic. It's just waiting for the Grand Chieftain to discover it should he dig too deeply." A very dangerous look comes over Gorren's face. "Do you have any idea what would happen if your imperious leader found this?"

Trollkin sent in the hundreds, the thousands, to dig it out. Rooms overflowing with gold. And then war. War between trollkin and humans would begin again, and go on endlessly until he destroyed humankind completely. We're only at a truce now because war is too expensive.

"He would have everything he wants," I say, more to myself than to Gorren.

"This is why we've been trying to stop them." The big orc replaces the lid on the pot and taps his map. "If they reach the well of magic underneath the mountain, then the world as we know it is over."

I frown. "There has to be a catch. This stuff isn't really *magic*. There's no such thing, and if there were, it wouldn't come without a catch."

"You're no fool, corporal." A hint of a grin twists his big lips, curling his tusks. "Magic has its limits. There is also one rather unfortunate side-effect to those who touch it."

I glance down at my hand, where I just held gold in my palm. "And what's that?" I ask, an uneasiness crawling up my spine.

Gorren cocks his head. "Well, it drives you mad."

"Huh?" I can't have heard him right. "What do you mean by *mad*?"

"My people are not the only ones to discover the existence of magic," Gorren says solemnly. His yellow eyes rise to mine, and there's a ferocity there that almost makes me shrink back. "You know of wild trolls of the jungle, don't you?"

There have always been stories about the wild trolls who make their homes near the trollkin city of Kalishagg—specifically their hunters, who will kill you, strip the flesh from your bones, and probably eat it afterwards.

Is that why they are the way they are? Because of magic?

"But you touched it," I murmur. And so did I.

At this observation, though, Gorren's smile grows wider. "Yes. Except that I have a human mate, you see." He chuckles. "A mighty fine one, at that. Owner of my heart and future mother of my whelps."

"And what does that have to do with anything?" I ask.

"It's only because of Vavi that I can wield this great power without risk." He tucks his hands behind his back and walks around the table. "It's because of her that I can be exposed to it and not lose my mind. Which is also the only reason I would ever permit you in here with it, corporal. Exposure to raw magic will drive a trollkin to insanity."

I touched the gold with my bare hand, and I have no such protection. Well, none greater than a lie, anyway.

Fuck. Who knows how long I have before the madness sets in.

"How do you know this?" I ask. "Humans and trollkin, mating, it's..." I stop myself. Do I really want to say that it's wrong? I don't think Gorren would appreciate hearing that.

"It was written!" The big orc puffs out his chest. "My people have been the guardians of these mountains for centuries. Deep in the rock there are caves where magic flows, and on these walls, our ancestors left behind messages for us."

One of the other two orcs in the room rises to his feet. "Imprinting between humans and trollkin is as old as history, corporal," he says to me with an impressive importance. "But war turns us against one another. We kill each other when we could be working together."

I almost roll my eyes. There is no great conspiracy behind why the Grand Chieftain and the human king send their soldiers into battle. It's greed, through and through. More land, more territory, more and more and more until the whole world is drained dry. Our only saving grace is the recent truce, but who knows how fragile that is?

The orcess who still remains sitting hums thoughtfully. "I don't need some words written on rock to tell me what my soul knows," she says, raising her eyes to mine. They are sharp, as if she sees that I'm an interloper. "I was led to my human. Magic drew me to him, and I will forever owe it a debt for that."

I have to hold in my scoff. *Magic* did such a thing? These orcs are all nuts.

"It must be a coincidence," I say. "I'm sure it has nothing to do with mating."

Gorren slaps me on the back. "Don't worry. You're safe here, with your Simka." Then he grows serious. "But now you understand why we'll do anything to prevent the Grand Chieftain from finding what's down there. That's why we need you to help stop him."

So this is why the orcs have come. This is why the mine has been under siege, and why they've stolen humans from their homes. It all makes sense now, much to my misfortune. If Gorren is telling the truth, who knows when this exposure to magic will drive me over the brink and turn me into one of the wild trolls, too?

What would happen to Simka then?

CHAPTER 12

SIMKA

When Jar'kel returns, his face is drawn and his eyebrows are pressed tight together. Even his blue skin looks pale.

"We need to leave as soon as possible," he says, fastening the tentflap closed behind him. He sits down next to me at the fire, so close I can smell him again, and it's that full, familiar smell I'm already growing so accustomed to. "This place isn't safe, not for either of us." He chews his bottom lip. "I've already put us in danger by accident. Gorren has a weapon. A dangerous weapon." As abruptly as he arrived, he gets up and relocates to the bed a few feet away from me. "Fuck. I might not be safe for you anymore, either."

I frown at the stream of nonsense coming out of his mouth. I've never seen him flustered before. "What are you going on about?"

Taking a deep breath, Jar'kel explains everything. The jar under the table. The magic he saw and touched with his own hands. The threat it poses to everyone in these mountains.

"So that's what Vavi meant," I say. "She sees herself as a guardian of magic. She thinks it's the reason the wild orcs brought her here, why she mated with Gorren. To protect it."

She also said that's why Jar'kel and I are here—to be protectors, too. But I know she's wrong. We aren't mates. We can't be what Gorren wants us to be.

"She's bought into it, too," Jar'kel says, his shoulders drawing up tight around his neck. "We need to get out of here, before something bad happens."

I think about what Vavi told me. Maybe she isn't so delusional after all, if there really is a threat as big as this hiding in the Blue Crags. "But what if they're right?" I ask. "What if the trollkin really are the biggest threat? If they discover this magic, it could be a disaster for—"

"I don't care!" Jar'kel's never raised his voice before, not like this, and I shrink back from it. "What becomes of them is of no concern to me. But I will not let myself fall to madness. And I won't let it happen to you, either!"

He's worried about me? A little bud of hope blooms in my chest thinking that perhaps, he feels some of the same pull that I feel.

"Did you find out about his next attack?" I ask. "If we're going to get out of here, we need to know when, so we can prepare."

"Not yet. I'm not in the inner circle." Jar'kel worries his broken tusk. "I need to give them something, or else they won't let me in."

I know he doesn't want to hand over the city guard's secrets, but he might not have a choice if we're going to get out of here. And if what Gorren's saying is true, there may be much more riding on our freedom than we thought.

We both look into the fire, neither of us speaking. If it were anyone else telling me this story, I wouldn't have believed it. But

Jar'kel is clearly disturbed by what he's seen, and I have to believe him.

That night, during dinner, he stays close to me. Like the night before, he puts his arm around me as we eat, but he doesn't attempt to touch me again—not like that.

I'm almost disappointed, because I liked how his hand felt on me, how warm his touch had been.

After the meal is over, though, and the other orcs start to retire to bed, my stomach does a flip. I know what Vavi and the others expect from us.

Back in our tent, Jar'kel secures the flap behind us. I put more logs on the fire, then make my way to the pile of furs in the back and sink into it. Jar'kel removes his coat and hangs it up, but leaves on his undershirt and pants. Then he gets into the bed next to me.

"You'll have to make a lot of noise," he says, and I don't think he likes this any more than I do. "Plenty of noise."

I nod. I heard the sounds my sister made at the celebration the other night. I think I can copy them.

"All right." I take a deep breath, steadying myself, and then let out a cry. Jar'kel jerks back, surprised.

"How was that?" I ask.

He groans and rubs his forehead. "Too sudden. More... pleased, less terrified."

"Oh." I try again, making a quieter noise, more like an animal. It comes out a strangled moan.

Jar'kel covers his ears. "Fuck," he grumbles. "Not like that, either. Surely you know what it should sound like?"

I block my face with my hands because I can't look at him. If he saw me right now, he'd know the truth.

Slowly, Jar'kel's four fingers wrap around mine, and he pulls them away from my face. "Simka." His expression is stern. "You *have* gotten under the blankets with someone before, haven't you?"

"Yes?" I squeak out. It doesn't look like he believes me, though. My shoulders sag as I finally say, "No."

He drops my hand like it's soiled. "Never?"

I shake my head. The opportunity just didn't arise. I was Vavi's little sister, the pest who was always getting in the way of more adult games. None of the village boys were interested me. No, they were all absorbed in learning their trades and swooning over prettier girls like Vavi. I was always too busy riding Fio and learning how to hunt.

Jar'kel lets out the deepest, most miserable sigh of them all, and he's a troll who sighs a lot. "You can't be serious."

"Should I try again?" I ask hopefully.

He groans. "I don't want them to think I've been beating you."

"I'll do it better this time," I say, resolute. I fall back on the bed, thinking hard about the orcs in front of the fire, a thick, wet cock sliding in and out of his mate's body. I remember the stream of white flowing down, how it made me feel warm, and strangely, hungry for Jar'kel.

I think of how I wanted to touch him. To see him. To kiss him.

Then I throw back my head and let out a moan.

JAR'KEL

This can't possibly be my life, sitting here listening to this.

Simka is a novice. She's never brought anyone inside her before. But the moan that comes out of her is, to my displeasure, rather convincing. It reaches my ears, travels down my throat into my chest, and finally, rests in my groin. My cock hears it and perks up.

The next time, she's much louder. I'm already drinking in the sound and growing thick under my pants.

"Is that better?" she asks breathlessly.

"Yes." It's all I can say. With a nod, Simka moans again, mixing it up with a gasping cry. This time it's even more realistic.

My entire body riots as even more pleasure leaks from her lips, filling the tent, echoing in the air around us. I squeeze my thighs with fingers so tight they're like claws, damning that snake between my legs. Fucking traitor.

Oh, how it wants her. How it longs to make her moan like that, even louder, even wilder. And it would be a real moan, a real cry of delight, as I took her nipples in my mouth and buried my cock inside her. Her strong legs would wrap tight around my hips as I took her, as I reached down and stroked her small, sensitive bead, as I turned her over and exposed her to me, licking her sweet cunt while my seed spilled out of her.

I'm hard as a stone now, but Simka is too lost in her performance to notice. As silly and inexperienced as she sounds, all it does is make me imagine if it were genuine as I brought her to a flying finish over and over again. She wouldn't just moan, but scream.

And she'd be screaming my name.

After a few minutes, Simka is breathing hard, her chest heaving up and down. She lifts her head and gazes up at me.

"Was that good?" she asks, eyes innocent and wide. She has no idea how much I'm hungering for her, *starving* for her. How could she?

I'm a fucking troll. An old, crotchety troll with one broken tusk and a mean streak a mile wide. She would never see me the way I see her.

"Yes," I say, and it comes out more choked than I'd intended. "It was... good." She blinks, and then before I can hide myself, her eyes travel down to my groin.

I spring to my feet, then stalk over to the rack where I keep my coat. I have to get out of here. I need something to take my mind off of what it would feel like to thrust inside her.

"Jar'kel..." Simka says uncertainly.

"What?" I snap.

She goes quiet for a moment as I put on the jacket and button it.

"Did you like it?" she asks.

I spin around to find her kneeling on the bed, one eyebrow quirked.

"No." I put a firmness in my tone I don't feel, not at all. "I can't help how my body reacts to a beautiful girl crying out."

Her lips turn up in a smile. "Beautiful?"

Oh, she's getting pleasure out of this all right. I growl rather than answering and head for the door. How she's making me feel —it isn't right. I have to get out of here before I do something I'll regret.

"You can't go out there," she says, stopping me in my tracks. "You were just inside me. Remember?"

At the suggestion, half the blood in my body rushes down to my cock, and the other half to my face. I desperately need some fresh air, but she's right. It's too suspicious.

I rub a hand down my face. "I can't do this anymore, Simka. I can't." The abject desire to wrap my arms around her, to kiss her, to touch every part of her, is overwhelming. Crushing me.

"Can't what?" she asks.

I whirl on her, my need turning into fury. "I can't pretend any longer!" I stalk towards her, every inch of my skin lit up. "I can't pretend we're together when we're not!" It's eating me up inside, this game, this lie, when what I want is for it to be true.

She bites her lip, and her soft, black eyes are bright. "Then why don't we stop pretending?"

My blood turns hot, so hot I almost can't hold myself back

from leaping onto the bed on top of her. She can't be saying what I think she's saying.

Damn it. The invitation is painfully appealing, because I need her. I need her so badly that if I stay here a moment longer, I might do something I can't take back.

"Come on." Simka gestures to the bed. "Don't run away."

"I'm not running," I grumble.

"You are running." She scoots aside, making room for me. "Let's just go to sleep. That's safe, isn't it? And then no one will talk if you don't go storming out into the camp."

She's right, and I hate it.

I sit down on the bed, dropping my head into my hands. I wish she'd never handed me the reins of that damned ass. I wish I'd turned her in when I saw her in the village. I wish I'd never seen that perfect, pert butt of hers climbing up the ice. I wish...

A pair of small hands reach around me. I stiffen as Simka leans her body against my back, and her deft fingers undo the top button of my jacket, then the next one, just by feel. I can't move, or even breathe. When she's finished, she tugs the coat down my shoulders, off my arms, and tosses it to the ground.

I have no choice. I can't stop myself as I turn around and find she has the furs open for me, waiting for me. Like a puppet on strings I crawl into them next to her. Perhaps this is the beginning of the madness, when I can no longer control my own actions.

It's when she slides towards me, lifting my arm and wrapping it around her, that my wretched cock wakes up again. I hold very still as she wedges herself tight against my chest.

My arms drape around her of their own accord, and I bring her close to my body. Her warmth seeps into me, filling me. A breath escapes my lips at the feel of her so close, at the rightness of it. She tucks her head under my chin, between my tusks, and her hand drifts up to trail down my cheek.

"Time for bed," she murmurs.

I simply nod, unwilling to move and end this moment. Almost immediately, she falls asleep.

Simka looks so peaceful, so sweet and small and perfect. I want to ball her up even tighter in my arms, squeeze her against me, slip inside her and make her cry out my name. I want to see her smile, to kiss her hard, to make sure she gets out of all of this safely.

Fuck. I should never have touched that gold in Gorren's hand. Wanting this human is insanity, and the madness has already started.

That's when I realize the truth.

It's finally come for me.

I squeeze my eyes shut and breathe through my nose, trying to calm myself. Not a human. Not this human, especially.

But the power of it, the knowing of it, rattles my bones.

She is mine. Without even a shred, not a tiny droplet of doubt, Simka is mine.

Does that mean I'm hers, too? The thought makes my teeth grind together. Does she feel what I feel? This aching, deep *want*, a need so powerful it overwhelms everything else?

Finally, I stop resisting and bundle her up even tighter, even closer. As much as I want to blame the magic for what's come over me, I can't deny that I've found her.

This young human woman is my mate. My only.

CHAPTER 13

SIMKA

There is no feeling in the world like falling asleep wrapped up by Jar'kel.

He may be rough, hard, and cold as a snow-covered stone, but there's a tenderness, too, hiding deep down inside. He refuses to look at it, to share it, but I know it's there, like a jewel waiting to be dusted off and treasured.

When I wake up, Jar'kel hasn't loosened his hold on me. His hips are firmly pressed against mine, that lump under his pants lurking at half-mast. I can't help wondering what he looks like down there. I tilt my head up to get a good look at him, and find him already looking back at me.

"Good morning," I whisper, even though the sun hasn't risen yet. The air is cold outside our cocoon of furs, so I keep every inch of myself hidden under them. I could get addicted to his warm body, even if there are a few layers of clothing between us.

He acknowledges me, but doesn't respond. The moment I curl tighter against him, he lets out a huff and his belly tenses. I think he's going to push me away, but instead he brings me in even closer, his leg pulling mine in between his and his chin tipping down to keep me wedged against his collar.

Nothing has ever felt so good as Jar'kel holding me this way, his chest rising and falling under my cheek. His hands roam across my body, but this time, there is no audience, no celebration, no bonfire. It's just the two of us here underneath the blankets. His warm fingers dance over the bare skin between my tunic and my pants, and he inhales sharply.

"Fuck." He buries his face in my hair, his tusk catching in the strands. I want to touch him all over—so I do, running my fingers up his chest, along the taut muscles of his neck, all the way to his ear. When I've explored the pointed tip of it, I continue down to his cheek. He stiffens when I approach his broken tusk, so I stop.

"You never told me," I whisper. "What happened."

"I didn't die is what happened."

This makes me chuckle. It's such a Jar'kel answer. I continue to the planes of his lips, which are softer than I expected. His breath hitches, and all I want is to taste him.

"They came at dawn," he begins, and my movement halts. "The bandits. I was working as a mercenary for a big merchant caravan. Everyone was just waking up, and the guard was changing. They came out of nowhere. Before I knew what was happening, someone was swinging an axe at my face."

I reach out and ever-so-gently rub my hand over the blunt, broken tusk. What's left cracked under the impact.

"It saved my life," he says, voice quiet. "The axe would have cleaved me right through my skull. While we were occupied, the rest of the band arrived, took what they wanted, and left like they were never there. I'm just lucky they didn't kill us all."

When I tilt my head up, trying to think of what to say, he's looking down at me, his face open to me, no longer hiding behind a high wall.

"I'm glad they didn't," I say.

Slowly, his hand rises to mine where it rests on his cheek, dwarfing it. His face tells me so many things that his words can't. Then, in one swoop, he ducks his head down and kisses me.

I've been kissed before, just as a part of silly children's games. I kissed Jar'kel, when we first agreed to our lie. But that was nothing like this.

His mouth instantly takes over, tugging me closer to him, opening my lips for his. He groans into me, and his hands slide up under my shirt, tasting me with the pads of his fingers.

Oh, his mouth. It's utterly and completely entrancing. He uses it in a way I never could have imagined, gently teasing my lower lip, sucking it in between his and releasing it again, his tongue tracing over the surface. I can't help a moan escaping as he plies me open, venturing even deeper, tasting me slow, sure and steady.

"You feel too good, Simka." His voice is strained and thick. He grabs my butt, hard, and pulls me in against him.

"You do, too," I hum in return. Now I can feel that lump under his breeches pressing into my thigh, and another moan escapes me at just the thought of it. I want to see it, right now more than ever. I want to see it, and touch it, and then perhaps, I want him to use it.

What would that feel like, to bring Jar'kel inside me the way Vavi did with Gorren? Oh. The idea of his thick cock sliding in and out of me, dripping with our wetness, makes me gasp, and Jar'kel groans against me in return. His hands travel up farther under my shirt, caressing every inch of my exposed skin, smoothing over my flesh and then squeezing it tight. When his fingers glance across the underside of my breasts, my body flexes against his, and he returns the pressure in kind, rubbing his hips against mine.

"Jar'kel," I murmur, and his hands stop abruptly. But I don't want him to stop, not ever. I want even more of him. "Should... should I take off my clothes?"

I think I've stunned him into silence. When his eyes never leave mine, all the hair on my body stands up on end with anticipation.

"Yes." It comes out of him a strangled whisper. "Take them off."

I fling away my shirt, then peel down my pants, and all the while Jar'kel is watching me, his gaze devouring me. When I'm finally naked in the blankets next to him, I'm tempted to cover myself, because his eyes are so intense. But I want him to see me. I want him to *want* me the way I want him.

He reaches out, his fingers gently landing on the dip in my collar bone at the base of my throat. From there, he trails them down to one of my breasts, following the curve of it. I've always wished my tits were bigger, like Vavi's, but there isn't a shred of disapproval on Jar'kel's face as he studies them.

It's a shock to my system when he brushes over my nipple. I can't help the sound that comes out of me as it sends a tingle straight up into my throat. His other hand smooths down my belly, rounded from the winter, to the gap between my legs. As he ventures to explore my other breast, his free hand ducks down to my thighs and urges them apart.

They obey without question. This is what I've wanted. This is what I've been craving. Gently his finger slips through, to the coarse hair at the base of my pelvis. I've touched myself, and sated my needs on my own, but never have I felt someone else there.

Jar'kel's eyes return to my face as his hand slips further down, tracing the inside of my thighs, teasing where he could be instead. But my body is hungry, hungry for something foreign. All I want is for him to dig deeper, to touch me where I desperately need to be touched.

His eyebrow quirks and his lip curls, like he can see exactly what I'm thinking. Then he leans down and takes my mouth in his again, right as he finally gives me what I want. One of his four thick fingers eases in between my folds, where I can sense an embarrassing moisture gathering. I clench my thighs, but he just groans with pleasure.

"Fuck, you're so wet." I take it this is a good thing. He swirls his finger around my entrance, gathering up all the liquid there, and travels up to the small pearl hidden under my hood—the place that always feels best when I rub myself in the night. He brushes over it, ever so slightly, and I moan into his mouth. It feels so good, better than good, better than my own hand could ever feel. He drags the pad of his finger across it again and again, until my moans are coming in a steady stream and my body is bucking against him.

He's good at this. I can't even control the noises I'm making, not this time.

Then he slides down again, and presses that finger inside me.

"Oh!" I throw my head back as it delves in, pulling me open, urging me to widen for him. It's new and yet glorious, like it was always meant to be this way.

"Ah," he says, nodding. "It's good you're a rider."

I blink up at him. "A rider?"

"Your cunt is already open." He slides in deeper, and I can't hold in my moan. *Cunt?* What a dirty word—but it lights me up hearing it from him. "I guess I have that mule of yours to thank. Otherwise, this would hurt a lot more."

"It definitely doesn't hurt," I say, and his lip curls in a smile.

His finger retreats, then slides in again, pumping in and out of me until I can feel myself dripping into his hand. Jar'kel's eyes are intense, focused only on my face as he leaves that slick cavern behind and returns to tormenting my clit. I curl into him, clutching his arm tight in my hands as the sensation takes me over, making my whole body tremble and shudder.

"Do you like that?" he asks, leaning his forehead against mine. All I can do is nod as moans and gasps tumble out of me. He speeds up, then slows his pace, bringing me higher and higher. The tension spreads all over, winding each of my muscles tighter as he moves faster, always gentle but still throwing tinder on the fire inside me. When he returns to my channel, I'm soaking wet, and his finger glides in and out easily before he once again goes back to rubbing me.

"Jar'kel," I manage between gasps as my hips snap against him. "That's so good." I'm clenching all over as a glorious sensation fills up every corner of my body. As much as I want to keep looking at him, I can't help closing my eyes as he moves faster, and faster, applying a steady, even pressure that's threatening to knock me over.

When I crest, it's as if the bonfire is burning here in our very tent, consuming me. I can't help crying out, and Jar'kel's hand speeds up, ratcheting my pleasure higher until I'm soaring through the air and the only thing keeping me rooted to the earth is the fact I'm gripping his arm tight.

Finally, he slows his attack, and I come crashing back to the ground. As I open my eyes again, he withdraws his hand and brings it up to his lips, inhaling the scent of me. Then his tongue darts out and licks it off his finger. It's mortifying, but his grin only spreads.

"Amazing," I manage between gasping breaths. I take his face in my hands and pull him in for another kiss, which he returns with a crushing fervor. I touch him all over, from his chin to his shoulders, down his chest and hips, taking in every part of him I can reach. When my hands land on his waist, though, he stops me.

I look up into his eyes. "Will you take off your clothes, too?" I ask, because all I want is to see him, to feel his tough skin under my hands. I want to see what else is under there, what even greater joys he can give me.

Jar'kel's eyes search mine, as if he expects to see doubt there. When he doesn't find it, he nods in assent, and sits up to peel off his shirt. Underneath, he's muscled, hardened by time. His blue skin is mottled with scars that each tell another story of his life. I want to touch each of them, to learn what they all mean.

"I'm keeping these on," he says, cinching the laces on his pants tighter, even though his cock is eagerly begging to be let out.

I furrow my brow. "Why? I want to see you."

He shakes his head. "No." When he returns to the bed, he takes me by the wrists and presses me down to the furs on my back, straddling me with his hips.

I pout. "Why not?"

"Because you're not ready yet." He kisses down my body, pausing when he reaches my nipple to pull one into his mouth. I can't help arching into him, and he chuckles—a sound I haven't heard him make before.

"But I am," I protest. "I am ready."

Jar'kel doesn't explain himself further as he teases my other nipple, and I've never felt anything as good. Instead of doing as I say, the stubborn troll, he trails his mouth down my belly, gripping my thighs to pull them apart.

"I'm going to devour you, Simka," he says in a low, rumbling voice. "I'm going to make you scream in so many ways, for many long years. But right now I'm going to eat you until all you can say is my name."

CHAPTER 14

JAR'KEL

M y mate tastes like everything I've ever wanted, everything I've needed my entire life. Her cunt is a well of tangy, salty bliss, and I can't wait to bury my tongue in it.

I'm no foolish whelp. I know that if I let her touch me, if I even let her see me, my control will be much harder to wrangle. Already my basest, purest instincts are begging me to bury my cock inside her and fuck her until she's screaming my name into the blankets. And then, once I'm surrounded by her wet, perfect heat, I'll spill as much of my seed inside her as I can, over and over.

Fuck. The mating bond is a piece of shit. This young girl doesn't need to be tied to me that way, bearing my whelps only for me to get even older and find my way into the ground. What about our offspring, who would lose at least one of their parents before they're even grown, the way I did? I had no one to lead me, to guide me, to help me find my way into the world.

No. I'm not going to stay in this awful, frozen place anyway. I have a home, and I'm going to return there when my job here is finished. If I don't plan to stay with Simka, if I deny the mating bond, it would be cruel of me to take away her first time in the blankets.

Not that I know what will happen when I leave and break the connection between us. I don't think anyone's ever tried it. Usually, finding your mate is... well, a cause for celebration, not an inconvenient side-effect.

The true madness lies in whatever great force paired me with Simka, so now I want nothing more than to fuck her until my whelp is growing inside her, to suck on her tits when they're heavy with milk and her ripe belly jiggles with every thrust. But I can't do any of that, so instead, I will give her the most pristine pleasure possible. I'll lick up her juices and fuck her with my hands and tongue until she doesn't hunger for anything more. And then I'm going to get us out of here, hides intact.

So, I pull my woman's sturdy thighs apart and drink in the smell of her, and there's nothing else like it. I crush my mouth into her warm, wet cunt, lapping at her with my tongue and sipping from her as she dribbles her desire.

"Jar'kel!" she moans, hips rising into my face. "Th-that's so... that's so..." I cut her off by sucking hard on her small bud. She writhes and moans, her thighs squeezing me, her hands curling in my hair. I'm frantic as I consume every part of her I can. When I slide my tongue into her, she's so small that I have to stretch her sweet cunt to fit, and I'm reminded again that she's never welcomed a cock inside her—probably never a mouth, either. I swirl it all around her tiny channel, drinking her up like the purest spring water and delighting in the thin hairs as they tickle my nose. The only thing in my head is her pleasure and wringing her dry of it.

Simka is crying out loudly as I sling her legs up over my shoulders, nursing her closer and closer to her pinnacle. Then I join my mouth with one finger, and oh, how much tighter she is now when I squeeze it inside her.

"Oh, fuck," she mutters as I pump it, curling it to stroke inside of her. Her hips snap hard, and her fingers dig into my hair. "Don't stop. Please. Please."

As if I would.

Then, she's clamping down hard around me, trapping my hand in her tiny cunt. Instead of crying out as I expected, Simka falls absolutely silent while her climax takes her over. When she reaches her stuttering finish, I don't stop, even as she tries to wriggle away.

"No," I growl, intent on my meal. My hand glides on a river of her ecstasy, in and out, as I lavish attention on her with my tongue. Simka's cries fill the tent, and again she seizes up around my hand, so tight I can barely move it. I can't stop from striking my own powerful finish inside my pants, her bliss washing over me like it's my own. Soon she's whimpering my name, begging me to stop.

It's not fair to her to sate my need this way, so I pull away harshly, letting her legs fall to the bed. My cock is a monster, fat and swollen despite the load I just unleashed, begging to be where it belongs. I sit up, breathing raggedly, while Simka's moans ebb. She's twitching all over, her breaths coming fast and hard, and my body is aching to be inside her soft, swollen cunt.

I can't stay here in this tent with her, crouched over her beautiful, naked body. If I do, then I'll go too far, and do something that can't be undone.

I'm about to get up and leave, to get far away from her as I can, when Simka nervously says, "Jar'kel?"

Fuck. I can't stand the worry in her voice, like she's done something wrong. So I pause, because the last thing I want is my mate thinking she's anything but perfect, anything but flawless in her beautiful moans and delicious body. I lie down next to her, then gather her up in my arms. Relief spreads across her face.

"What was that?" Simka asks hoarsely. At least now she finally knows how to scream. "What did you do to me?"

"It was nothing," I tell her, pulling her close and burying my face in her soft, short hair. My cock is in agony, but I am its master.

"Nothing?" she asks with a laugh. "Didn't feel like nothing."

I wish I could tell her that it was, that the true pleasure I could bring her is far beyond that, but she'll never know. No, I can't be with her in the true way and then walk away from her. I can't be her mate, start a family with her, and curl around her every night —not when I can't live her whole life with her, not when I may not see our whelps to adulthood.

That only ends in misery for us and for them.

I had hoped this would sate me, but now I hunger for nothing more than Simka. I have to breathe hard just to shove down my need.

Tomorrow, I have to cut this off. I can't let it grow even further and take over me like an infection, or we'll never be free of each other.

And she deserves to be free of me.

SIMKA

Damn. I won't be the same again, not after that.

Jar'kel really knew what he was doing down there, that much is for sure. Is it because of his age, or was he just born knowing his way around my body like he drew the map himself?

I feel boneless, liquefied, utterly drained in the best possible way. The sloppy, wet sounds he made between my legs should have been horrifying, but it only drove me higher into the clouds.

But something feels off. Why wouldn't he let me see him or touch him? Why did he tense up, as if to flee?

I feel selfish. I want to please him as much as he pleased me. When I run my hand down his body, I find the front of his pants soaking wet.

"Simka," he chides me, pulling my arm away to wind it around his middle instead.

"What?" I'm only curious.

"Your cunt tasted so fucking good that I went off." The words shoot like fire through me. I did this to him? "That's all I need. So go back to sleep."

I feel like he's hiding something from me, though, and I don't like it. I want to interrogate him more, to find out what's missing and why he won't show himself to me when I showed everything to him, but I'm so tired now. All I want is Jar'kel's body close to mine, his heart beating next to my ear.

Pressed against his bare chest, I wander away into the warm darkness of his arms.

But when I startle awake, I'm strangely cold.

I'm never cold—this is my home, the place where I was born and raised, and no cold is too cold for me. But something is clearly missing, and my body knows it.

Jar'kel is gone, and the place where he'd been beside me is empty and creased in the shape of him. I blink a few times to clear the fog of sleep, wondering if I imagined what happened in the darkness of the early morning. It's bright outside now, and I sit up abruptly in bed, looking around for any sign of my troll.

I rub the side of my head, trying to place this feeling of emptiness. After what he did last night between my legs, I don't know what to make of his absence. Did I offend him? Does this have something to do with how he refused to show himself to me, while I laid bare like an offering?

The need to see him, to feel his arms around me, is over-whelming. My heart starts to race. Something feels wrong, as if Jar'kel has been with me my whole life and now suddenly he's not. I want to find him and drag him back to bed where he belongs: with me.

But he must not want the same thing, and that's why he left without waking me. Did he lick me so thoroughly just to make our ruse believable? Or was it just to sate his own needs, to use me for his own pleasure? We did something so intimate together, but it was all one-sided.

Wait. This burning desire to have him near me... It's all sudden, very sudden. *Too* sudden. I've never been dependent on anyone. I hunt for my family and see to my own needs. And I definitely don't want Jar'kel. No, I shouldn't be lusting for a grouchy old troll like him. I shouldn't crave him around me, inside me, filling me up, encompassing me while a cold wind blows around us. It's senseless.

Something has changed me, in a deep and profound way, and I'm terrified of how visceral it is. Whatever has happened, I know that somehow, it's his fault.

I throw my clothes on and storm out of the tent. What was so damn important that he had to leave?

Gorren. Jar'kel is trying to sneak his way into the orcs' circle and find out their plans. That's all he cares about—escaping this place—and what we did means nothing to him.

When I reach the leader's tent, I'm so overcome with my fury that I tear the flap as I open it. Gorren glances up from his seat where Vavi is perched on his lap. Two other orcs nearby are poring over a leather map, while Jar'kel stands with his arms crossed. When I stomp inside, his eyes go wide.

"Simka?" Vavi asks, hopping up. "What are you doing here?"

"You." I ignore my sister as I point at Jar'kel. "What have you done to me?"

His lips part, and his eyebrows fly into his hairline. Then he scowls. "What are you talking about?"

I'm in front of him before I even command my feet to move, glaring up into his face. "The moment I woke up and you were gone, I—" I choke on the words as I remember how frightened and alone I was, and how full of rage I am now. He's turned me into someone I don't recognize.

For a split second, the deep wrinkles on Jar'kel's face ease, and he looks almost like he pities me. "You feel it, then?"

I level my full outrage on him. "Feel what? Tell me what you did to me!"

He takes a long, deep breath, like I've already tired him out. "You think I want this?" he asks quietly. "You think I *want* to be tied to a human? To a silly, foolish, headstrong girl like you?"

Is that how he sees me? It splits me open like the sweep of a sword.

"But... all those things you did," I say, my voice quavering. I'm vaguely aware of the other orcs, of Vavi in the same tent, but they fade into the background. "Now I'm just a silly girl?"

Jar'kel doesn't flinch, and his eyes are as hard as stone. "That is what you are, isn't it? Barging in here and making a fool of yourself." His frown deepens, making more creases around his mouth. "I didn't ask for this, either, you know. Being mated to you."

"Mated?" I echo, my voice shrinking. He can't mean what I think he means. "But... it's not..."

He sighs wearily, like this is all a very annoying, childish game. "Yes. You're my mate, Simka, and I'm yours." His voice is dark with disappointment. "It's not something we choose. It's something that's done *to* us."

The moment he says it, I know it to be true. I remember what Vavi said—*he's my everything, and I'm his, too.*

Jar'kel is mine. *Mine.* He belongs to me and no one else. Now I understand the avalanche of fury and hurt washing over me. My soul has been taken from me and bound up with his, and it's rioting.

"The bond is awful, isn't it?" he goes on. "To be tied to someone you hate?" He lets out a low, self-deprecating laugh.

Goosebumps spread across my skin, and my rage twists into something else, something worse. "You hate me?" I back away, putting distance between us, as the truth settles on my shoulders.

He doesn't care about me. He didn't pleasure me because he *likes* me. That's why he wouldn't show me his body, and why he left as soon as he could. He only did it because instinct made him. Because of the stupid bond.

"Just because we're mates doesn't mean we have to accept it," Jar'kel says, his tone cutting, his face not showing a shred of emotion. "It doesn't have to mean anything if we don't want it to."

But I wanted it to mean something, I realize. I wanted to wake up next to him, to feel his arms around me, to revel in his touch. I wanted to be let inside. Being his mate could have been a wonderful thing.

But he fucking hates me.

"Simka," Vavi says, reaching out to me. I'd forgotten anyone else was even in the room with us. I can't believe he's doing this, *here*, in front of everyone.

I slap her hand away and grit my teeth to hold in my tears. "Don't you dare," I hiss at her. "This is your fault. You're the one keeping us here. You're the one who won't let me leave again, who threatened to kill him if I didn't—"

I stop myself. I can't reveal the pact we made, the secret we've been keeping. But I can't stay here anymore, either, where Jar'kel watches me with eyes as hard as flint. My whole body is hot and blistering with my humiliation.

He was my lifeline. I thought there was something tender, something still small but growing between us, but I was painfully wrong. Now we're lashed together like two logs of a boat in a thunderstorm, two beings who couldn't be more different.

I have to get out of here. I have to get as far away from him as I can before he gets an even tighter hold on me. And I can't stand another second in this fucked up place.

Instead of saying anything else to him, I turn and sprint from the tent. I don't go back to our fire, to our bed. No, I'm desperate for something familiar, anything that makes sense. I run past tent after tent, heading toward the edge of the camp. I need to go home. I need to see Dad. I'm fast, and I know the snow, and I know this land.

I careen past orcs going about their daily business, heading for the ridge that leads back the way we came. Maybe if I'm quick enough on my feet, I'll have the element of surprise and a good shot at making it out of here alive.

He hates me. He's supposed to be mine, and he fucking *hates* me.

I reach the rocks that surround the valley and blaze past them, pouring all of my misery into my legs. I beg them to carry me out of here.

Suddenly, a dark shape leaps out, tackling me to the ground. I gasp as I hit the snow on my belly, and a heavy body lands on top of mine. Someone grabs my arms, wrenching them behind my back, and I cry out.

"Let me go!" I shout, twisting and squirming, trying to free myself. But whoever has me is much stronger. My captor mutters something in Trollkin, and drags me up to my feet. Tears of rage and misery are streaming down my face as the big orc tosses me over his shoulder.

All I can think as he carries me sobbing back to the camp is how Jar'kel will mock me for once again being a foolish, stupid girl.

CHAPTER 15

JAR'KEL

Simka's devastated face will forever be burned into my memory.

I've heard of this, the emotional rollercoaster that comes with new matehood. The bond must have settled on her this morning, igniting into a flame when she woke up to find me gone. She had no understanding with which to fight it.

I should have stayed. I should have explained to her what was at stake, but I thought if I offered Gorren something tangible, I might learn what I need to know—and then we could get out of here before she imprinted on me, too.

Now it's much too late.

I didn't run after her. Either she'll escape and run all the way home, back to her father and her village, or someone will catch her trying. I'm not surprised when one of the orcs guarding the edge of the camp appears, dragging a howling woman back to our tent. She hisses like a cat and claws at him, demanding to be released.

She is a wild animal, barely contained as the irritated orc hauls her through the mud.

When I finally see her face, it's red and streaked with tears, and deep inside me, something breaks. My Simka, as feral as she is beautiful, as fierce as she is soft inside. When the orc sees me, he thrusts her against me.

"Take your fucking woman," he growls. "If she tries to get away again…"

The fact that she is Vavi's sister may not save her. I nod and grab Simka around the middle, all while she thrashes.

"Fuck you!" She spits right on my face. "Just let me go!"

"No," I say calmly, lifting her off the ground and carrying her under my arm into the tent. I secure the flap closed and toss her onto the bed so she can calm down. I think she's going to try to flee again, but instead, she falls still where she landed. Then, after a few seconds of silence has passed, Simka curls up tight in a ball.

I want her to say something to me. I want her to scream at me, at least, and tell me how she feels about what I've said. I deserve it, whatever comes out of her mouth. It was cruel, I know. She should get her rage out now, so she can move on with her life later, after I'm gone. I've done what I can to make that possible.

Instead, she lies there, not moving or making a sound. Every instinct in my body is pulling me towards her, demanding I comfort her, apologize to her, tell her that she means more than anything in this whole damned world to me. But it wouldn't be fair, not when I've told her in no uncertain terms where we stand.

It's much better this way.

I sit down on the edge of the pile of furs, just far away enough I won't be tempted to touch her. Simka's little body is shaking, but I hear no sobs, no tears. That's good, at least, that her strength has protected her this much.

"You can't escape like that," I tell her. "You'll only make it worse."

"I know." Her voice isn't sad or angry. It's simply there, full of nothing. Empty.

"You won't try again? Not until it's safe, and we've made a plan?"

She shakes her head, never once looking up. "I won't."

"That's good," I say. When she offers nothing else, I decide that I have to get away from her or I won't be able to stop myself from drawing her into my arms and squeezing her tight until I've drained all her sadness away.

When I'm outside the tent, I find Vavi approaching, her arms wrapped tightly around herself.

"Corporal," she murmurs. "They found her? They brought her back?"

I nod.

Her head droops. "Were the two of you lying to me all along?"

I nod again.

"But now... it found you. Didn't it?" But she already knows the answer, so I don't speak. "Well, I hope you'll treat her well."

"It should have never happened," I say. "It shouldn't have picked us. It shouldn't have picked *me*."

"Too bad." Her eyes are so like Simka's that it makes my stomach flop over when she narrows them, scrutinizing me. "Now it has happened. So what are you going to do about it?"

When I say nothing, Vavi *tsks* and steps into the tent without another word.

But she doesn't understand. She doesn't realize I'm doing what's best for Simka, for her future offspring. They'll never have to know the life that I did without a father.

Besides, refusing the bond won't hurt her the way it will me. She's human. She's safe, and she won't suffer once the sting has worn off.

This is what's right, even if it carves out a hole in my chest.

SIMKA

I'm stuck with him. Or rather, he's stuck with me.

I could have tolerated it. I could have come to love Jar'kel rather easily, I think. All the bits and pieces are there, but none of them will come together without his heart, and I'm not sure he has one.

After I hear some talking outside, Vavi comes into the tent and sits down next to me. I only burrow deeper under the furs.

"You know, I wasn't always happy here," she says, gently stroking the blanket on top of me. "It took time for my bond with Gorren to develop, for us to see eye-to-eye. But look at us now."

I ignore her.

"Jar'kel's struggling too, Simka. He just shows it in a different way. He'll come around."

When I don't answer, she rubs my shoulder once more and then leaves.

At last, I'm alone. No one bothers me for the rest of the day as I lie in bed, hating myself as much as I hate Jar'kel, and this camp, and my sister for trapping us here.

I'm awoken the next morning by the smell of someone bringing in food. The fire has died, so the orc who deposits my tray on the rickety table sets about to relighting it. I wave her off.

"It's fine." I don't think she can understand me, but she gets the message and leaves with a pitying look. Does everyone here know now that my mate has thrown me away?

Reflexively I divide the food in half, then realize Jar'kel is probably getting his meals elsewhere, and decide to eat the entire thing myself. When I'm so full I feel sick, I crawl back into the bed and lie there for what feels like hours, staring up at the stretched leather roof of the tent.

Eventually I get up, after the sun has already set, and peer outside. There's a bonfire burning in the gathering area, and I slink down the rows of tents to get a look at what's going on. Unlike the last celebration here, there's a somber air around the camp. Vavi waves at me when I appear, and walks over with her bow-legged gait.

"What's going on?" I ask.

"Raid tomorrow," she says, and I don't miss the hint of fear in her eyes. She puts her hands on my shoulders and takes stock of me from head to toe. "You've been so cooped up. Why don't you come sit with us?"

I catch sight of Jar'kel's blue hair on the other side of the fire, where he's drinking mead and staring into the flames. He hasn't noticed me yet, so I back away into the shadows.

"Sorry," I tell my sister. I can't even stand to look at him—it hurts too much.

Vavi gazes at me with a sad kind of pity that I hate. "I'd really hoped this would all turn out differently," she says. I know she fantasized about us having children who could play together, but that will never be in my future. Perhaps she and Gorren were destined for one another, but Jar'kel's right, and a mistake was made with us. As if I would ever have children with a monster like him.

"Me too," is all I say. I'm trapped here now, thanks to her. I should never have agreed to Jar'kel's proposal and come looking for her.

I miss Dad and Fio now more than ever.

I go back to the tent, my chest so heavy it feels like it will crush me into the earth and I'll never get up again.

JAR'KEL

Simka appeared at the gathering, but only for a moment to exchange words with her sister. I tried not to acknowledge her, hoping that she might stay for a while. It's not good for her to be holed up in the tent like she's been.

Instead, she vanishes as soon as she appears, and a stone sinks into my belly. More than anything I want to go to her, to repair the broken fence between us, but my feet stay solidly put. I can't take back the words I said, the ones that crushed her in front of my eyes. I have to carefully maintain this wall erected between us to keep the mate bond out. I've never heard of a trollkin trying to ignore it before, but then again, it's not like many of us have imprinted on humans.

Then I think of the orc lieutenant and his human captain, who both gave up everything to be with each other—to try to find happiness in a world that didn't want them to be happy. I don't want that for Simka.

I drink more as I watch Vavi on Gorren's lap, his arms wrapped tight around her belly, whispering something in her ear that makes her giggle and blush. They're like teenagers, and it looks foolish on a grown orc like him. But even the night before an ambush, when they'll all be risking their lives for what they believe in, he's smiling and nipping her neck. After a time, she takes his hand and they leave the bonfire, and not long after I can make out the sound of Vavi's pleasure echoing around the camp.

Two mugs of mead later, I stumble back to the tent that Gorren assigned to me. He was the one who suggested I keep my distance in hope that Simka won't try to escape again. The dwelling is small and reeks of animal, but at least I'm alone there.

My body, on the other hand, isn't so keen to be away after

getting a taste of her. All I have to do is remember the scent of her cunt, the flavor of her pleasure on my tongue, and I'm hard as a log. I take my cock and stroke it mercilessly, imagining how it would feel to be buried inside her, until my seed splatters across my chest. In disgust, I wipe it away with a blanket.

It doesn't sate my need, though, and I fall asleep with the memory of Simka's moans echoing in my dreams.

The next morning, before they depart, Gorren pulls me aside. He's dressed in thick armor with two blades at his hip. He and his people won't stand a chance if all they have is swords against the city guards' guns, but he looks more than confident.

"Corporal." The massive orc's voice is unforgiving, and there's no lightness to him. "The train schedule. When will the next one be arriving to pick up ore?"

I know the answer to his question, of course. But I'm not going to offer up the city guard on a silver platter.

"I don't know," I say. "Wasn't my job to keep track of trains."

He sighs and shakes his head. "Vavi's sister means a lot to me," he begins carefully. "And as her mate, I've been patient with you. But my patience is running thin, and you don't want to know what happens when I finally lose it."

A shudder travels down my spine. If he killed me, what would happen to Simka?

When the wild orc forces depart on their mission, they leave additional guards behind, probably to keep her from running again. I realize now how much I've fucked my own scheme. I had hoped we could get out of this prison and then go our separate ways, but now our position is worse than ever.

Simka avoids me, never once leaving her tent for the three days the attack force is gone. I wonder if she's eating well, if she's getting any exercise, if she's managing to sleep when I can barely get a lick of shut-eye. All I can think about when I lie back in bed is the sound of her moans, the warmth of her body against mine, the taste of her sweet, brown nipples in my mouth. I imagine her dark eyes, the roundness of her face, how she lights up when she smiles —smiles that are so rare, smiles that she gave me.

Every one of my instincts is hating me, but my mind knows better. Maybe I'll be miserable for the rest of my life, but that's better than stealing her innocence and binding her to a jaded old man who will die before her whelps are even grown. It's better than her young life ending too soon.

I have to keep telling myself this, or I won't be able to stay away.

CHAPTER 16

SIMKA

After Vavi was taken and I lost the wild orcs' trail, I cried all night, sometimes all day, missing my sister—and my best friend. She meant the world to me, and then she was gone.

Was she still alive? That thought kept me awake for days on end, turning me into a ghost of myself. I couldn't be there for Dad, as miserable as I was, and he was too distraught to be there for me, either. We co-existed, trying to muddle our way through our grief together. It was up to Fio to comfort me, and I spent many days and nights petting his soft, thick fur, or riding around the countryside hoping I would spot an elk so I could feel worthwhile.

Somehow, being apart from Jar'kel is nearly as awful. It feels like a part of me has been ripped loose and is now floating away, while I try desperately to bring it back.

I don't cry. Crying is for the weak. I remain hard, and eat my food, and stay inside my tent where no one can witness how pathetic I am. When the orcs leave for their raid, Vavi is alone and worried about Gorren's safety, but I can't be there for her. I can't comfort her like she needs.

Has Jar'kel found a way out like he promised? If he does, will he escape in the night and abandon me? Unlike Jar'kel, I've proven myself to be a flight risk, so often I look outside my tent to find an orc standing not-so-subtly nearby. There's no chance I'll be getting out of here anytime soon.

I wait the next day for news that he's fled in the night, but I hear nothing. Meals continue to be brought to me in silence, and I only eat occasionally. There's no need to consume much when I'm not moving my body. Often I don't even light the fire, and I simply hide in my bed under the furs trying to sleep because it's easier than being awake. I simply have no energy to do anything, like it's all been sapped from my body. The pull towards Jar'kel is sharp and powerful, and everything else fades into the background as I resist it.

At night, I reach down between my legs and touch myself, hoping to relive the moment he licked me to my blissful explosion. I close my eyes and imagine him there, tongue lashing my clit, his finger pumping in and out of me. But nothing I do can even compare.

I wonder if it will always be this way, wishing I'd never seen him outside city council that day, craving him and hating him with all of my heart.

JAR'KEL

During the day, I wander the camp, pretending to be stretching my legs while I take stock of our surroundings, cataloguing where the guards tend to position themselves.

It hasn't escaped my notice that there's now a guard posted

outside her door. Perhaps I could escape on my own, but taking her with me... that would be a significant challenge now.

I can't do that. I can't leave her here while I find my freedom. I may be a selfish bastard, but I wouldn't abandon her that way. So I sit at one of the tables around the fire pit, waiting and watching as the world goes by and the snow falls on our heads.

When the orcs return, they're bloodied and fewer in number. Over the ridge, Gorren appears carrying the head of a troll in his hand. He raises it up high and roars, and the rest of the orcs roar back. Their mission, to take out the load destined for transport on the train, must have been successful. Vavi races out to greet him, and he tosses the head to the ground as he lifts her up into the air, swinging her around.

Despite those they lost, that night there is a great celebration, even more raucous than the one the orcs held when Simka and I arrived. The troll's head is mounted on a pike and planted near the fire, and I even catch one orc whipping out his cock and pissing all over it. I've seen some foul things in my time, but another troll's face staring back at me whenever I look up at the bonfire drives a stake through me, too. That could be me if I don't start working with Gorren soon.

But can I betray my people that way? Can I really sacrifice them so I can live?

I'm surprised to see Simka there, sitting to the left of her sister, her eyes trained on the ground. I've taken a seat at one of the farther tables, near the edge of the gathering, drinking my mead. Most of the orcs are here celebrating, but a few have remained standing guard. If there's one thing I've learned in my military years, it's that soldiers are still ordinary individuals who crave companionship. Perhaps I can learn something useful from them to help us get out of here.

Being careful not to look in Simka's direction, I pick up a few extra mugs and fill them with mead, then carry them to the edge of the camp. I can feel Gorren's gaze on me, following me as I walk out to the ridge where I know the guards are hiding.

"Brought you something," I call out. One of them emerges, a suspicious look in his eyes.

His lip curls. "What's this?"

"Well, you can't partake in the party, so I thought you might want something anyway." I shrug. "I used to be a member of the city guard. I've been where you are, watching the world go by while you stand watch."

He nods, still uncertain, but he seems more open to my offer. He takes the mug and swigs it, and I sit down on a rock nearby to make conversation.

"What really brings you here?" the orc asks, surveying me carefully as he drinks. Another has joined us, leaving his post.

I shrug. "What I said."

"Mmhmm."

The second orc pipes up. "Avoiding your mate still?" he asks.

No point lying about it if everyone already knows now. "Yes." I take another drink, uninclined to explain.

He furrows his brow. "Why? I'd be over the moon to have a human mate." He says it like I'm an idiot.

"No, you wouldn't. It's terrible." I laugh a self-deprecating laugh. "I assure you, they're very difficult creatures." Mine is as difficult as she is enchanting, unfortunately.

"The others say they have the smallest, tightest holes you've ever felt," the first orc says, slugging back his mead. "And the bond —they feel it just as much as we do, if not more."

I scowl. "No, they don't," I say with certainty. "Only trollkin do."

"You've seen Gorren's little human," the orc says with an envious chuckle. "She worships him. I wouldn't mind some of that myself, you know. A sweet human to miss me while I'm gone, and warm my bed when I get home? I'd never let that go." He looks wistful, but my blood is turning cold. "They most certainly feel it, corporal."

I clench the handle of my mug tight. I thought my suffering was limited to me, that I was the only one feeling the pain of our separation. Simka might be sad for a time, but it would be temporary. Nothing like the abject misery I feel now.

But if Simka is experiencing something even close to this... The surface of my mead ripples as my hand shakes.

"Why don't you want her?" the second orc asks me, finishing off his drink. "She's pretty, for a human."

I don't like the tone of his voice as he talks about my woman. The word flies through my thoughts before I can stop it.

My woman. Mine. Only mine.

I glare at him as I say, "Pretty or not, it won't work between us. I'm too old for her."

He holds his hands up in surrender. "Not planning to creep on your territory," he says. "But someone else might, if she's not up your alley."

"And she probably doesn't care how old you are, if the mate bond has a hold on her." The other orc sits down on the rock across from me. "I doubt she cares about anything but having you there."

"Not to mention your cock," snorts his companion. They go on chatting about how the other humans in the camp have fallen deep into the crevasse of matehood, following their own orcs around like puppies. The guards' lips are growing looser by the moment, and this could be my opportunity—but all I can think about is whether or not they're right.

Is Simka going to spend her life feeling as empty, as unfinished, as I do now? Will she also feel as if her heart is rotting in her chest? I shiver at the thought.

"If I had a little mate like that, I wouldn't treat her nearly as bad as you do yours," the first orc says to me.

"It's better this way," I snap, though even I don't believe myself anymore. "If she hates me, the bond won't affect her when I die."

One of the guards snorts out a laugh. "You really think that? It's a done deal, corporal."

The other orc shakes his head. "If she didn't hate you before, she sure does now."

The sheer magnitude of my cruelty washes over me. He's right. If Simka is truly imprinted on me the way I am to her, how much have I been torturing her by ignoring her? By sleeping in another tent, by pushing her away?

I think of the agonizing, endless aching in my chest, and I'm nearly drowned in my guilt. I did this to spare her the pain, not to inflict it on her.

Getting back to my feet, I sway a little bit from all the mead I've had, my legs soggy underneath me. Just great. I won't be fleeing here anytime soon. I'm an idiot, through and through, throwing away every good chance I've had. But maybe I can still course-correct on one of my mistakes—or try to.

I stumble back to the celebration, intent on finding Simka and doing... something. Something to cross the vast chasm between us, to heal all the hurt I've inflicted on her. I search and search the faces around the fire, but she's not there. For a moment my mind panics that she's made an escape again.

"Looking for someone?" asks Gorren. He leans his head on one hand, elbow propped on the arm of his big chair with Vavi sitting in her permanent place on his lap. "She left."

Fuck. I thought it would be easier to talk to her with others around, because she might be less inclined to simply hit me in the face. I need her to listen to me without trying to kill me.

But the mead is telling me to go, so I dip my head to Gorren and head off into the camp, my feet carrying me on instinct towards Simka. When I reach the tent, the flap is tied closed with two stiff knots. I don't know how she plans on leaving in the morning.

Maybe she doesn't intend to.

I set about removing them, until I get frustrated with my clumsy hands and I tear apart the leather straps, instead. I yank open the tent flap and step inside.

The fire is out, and it doesn't look like it's been lit in days. There are trays of half-eaten food on the floor and table, and clothes scattered around. Someone is lying in the bed, buried under the furs.

"I'm not in the mood, Vavi," comes an irritated voice from underneath. She pokes her head out. "Just go—"

She freezes when she sees me standing there. Then a terrible rage comes over her.

"What are you doing here?" she snarls, sitting up and pulling the furs tight against herself.

"I wanted to—" I begin.

"Get the fuck out." I have never seen one small person look so absolutely furious. She might just murder me with her eyes.

"Simka, please listen to me." I didn't have a plan when I came in here, but right now, I'll say anything to erase that look from her face, the one that says I have cut her down to the sinew and she'll never forgive me for it.

"No!" She gets up holding the fur around her, and I wonder what she was doing in here alone. Is she naked under there? "Get out of my tent right now, *Jar'kel*."

The way she says my name like a curse eats at my soul.

"I'm not leaving until you listen to me." I try to keep my tone soothing. "Please."

Simka is shivering with her rage and the sadness she keeps buried underneath it. "I'm not listening to a single thing you have to say, asshole." She snatches a dagger out from under the bed, where she must have been hiding it. Surely they would've taken it from her if they knew she had it.

I have well and truly fucked everything, I realize, as she stalks towards me with the point aimed at my heart. "Get out," she says between clenched teeth.

"Simka." I stand my ground, because hell, if she wants to kill me, who am I to stop her? If I die by anyone's hand, it should be hers. "I know I've been... horrible."

She barks out a laugh. "Horrible? Does horrible really cover it, though?" She takes a step towards me, until the point of the dagger is pressed against my chest. It digs a hole in my coat, twisting until it reaches my skin.

"Do it," I hiss at her, losing every last shred of my self-preservation. "Stab me. Hit me. Anything that means you still feel something for me."

CHAPTER 17

SIMKA

Jar'kel is daring me to slide my dagger through his ribcage, and I'm tempted to do it. After everything he's said to me, how he used me and threw me away, I find that I want to kill him just as much as I want his arms around me. I long to never see him again as much as I crave his lips on mine.

How does this one asshole troll make me feel so much? It's the most bruising punishment possible for him to be standing here in front of me, asking me to bare my bleeding soul to him.

"Do it," Jar'kel says again, leaning even closer, so the tip of my blade presses into his skin and draws a pinprick of blood. His cool composure has melted, leaving behind something vulnerable and pained, and I can see a reflection of my own suffering on his face as clearly as I feel it in my gut. "I know you hate me," he says quietly, "more than anything. So why not?"

The misery in his voice is a mirror to my own. But what does he have to pity himself for? He put up this barrier between us. He's the one pushed me away and discarded me like garbage.

"Why not?" My voice goes high pitched and tight. Of course I want to hurt him as he's hurt me. "Because I... I..."

I can't say it. The ugly truth is that I need Jar'kel more than air to breathe, but I can't give him that power over me. Not when he can so brutally injure me with it.

"Because you feel it, too?" he says, his words tinged with hope. "This aching hunger?"

I can't deny that it's consumed me, how badly I've wanted him back in this tent like he is now. Already my heart is hammering and my skin is warm, and I want nothing more than to collapse into his arms.

"I do," I finally say, trying to keep in the tears. I can't even lie to him—that's the hold he has on me. "I feel it, too. But I can't love someone who despises me."

His lips part, and the deep crease between his brows fades. I can't stop the tears anymore. They burst free in a powerful stream, flooding down my cheeks.

"I can't help it," I say, the words coming out as a sob. "I want to hate you back. I want you to go jump off a cliff, but just the thought..." I turn away from him so he can't see me break. I wipe my face frantically, trying to stop the flow. "Please go away. Please stop torturing me like this. I never want to see you again, Jar'kel. Not ever."

A soft hand lands on my shoulder. Just the touch of his four fingers on my bare skin makes my soul sing, but I shake him off and back away. I won't let one gentle touch erase what he's done.

"I'm sorry, Simka." Jar'kel's voice breaks as he sinks down to his knees, right in front of me. "For saying what I said. For putting you through this. I'm so, so sorry." His head drops to his chest. "I want you. I *need* you. I've needed you for so long, before I even met you."

What? I don't understand.

"Then why—" I choke on it as it comes out. "Why would

you...?" I won't forget how cold his eyes were as he told me exactly how he felt about me, how he tore me open with just a few words.

Jar'kel takes a halting breath, still unable to meet my eyes. "Because I can't do that to you. I can't steal your first time in the blankets. I can't fill you up with whelps the way every part of me wants, or I'll take you down with me."

His shoulders are trembling as he reaches out and wraps his hands around my legs, then sinks against me. His touch sends a ripple of pleasure through my entire body. "I can't bind you to me knowing I'll just leave you while you're still young. Knowing I'll want nothing more than to have a family with you, only to abandon them when I..." His voice catches, and he can't utter the last word.

Oh. Suddenly, I understand. It crashes over me like a tidal wave on the rocky shore, knocking over everything in its path.

Jar'kel does want me. He wants me, but can't bear to hurt me. To *leave* me, when his life someday comes to an end.

"When I go, Simka," he says, voice barely above a whisper, "there's a good chance you'll go, too. What then? I can't do that to you, or to *them*."

If he thinks I'm afraid of some far-off thing like that... I huff with frustration. Why couldn't he have told me the truth? Why did he have to put us both through this?

"We can't live in fear!" His head jerks up at my reprimand, and his eyes are wet around the edges. "Anything could happen to us in the future, Jar'kel. I could get mauled and eaten by a bear. You could fall into a trapper's pit and never come home. But we still have to live our lives. If you spend every day thinking it might be your last, you'll never have a chance to be happy."

It's as if he doesn't understand the word. "Happy?" His brow creases. "There's no way this ends in happiness for either of us. I'm a dead-end for you."

What's happened in his long life to make him believe he can't have joy? That he doesn't deserve it?

"What if I want the chance?" I ask him, and my voice breaks. "Even if it ends someday, what if... what if I want to live what life we have together?"

His grip on my legs tightens. "Simka, you don't want this. You don't want *me*. I will ruin you."

But I'm not some sweet creature whose innocence he has to protect.

"What if I want you to ruin me?" I ask quietly, reaching down to stroke his hair. His eyes grow huge.

"You can't mean that." Jar'kel's grip on me tightens. "You don't know what you're asking for."

I'm tired of this, of him pushing me away. If he won't cross the chasm between us, then I will.

"Get up," I demand. Confusion flashes across his face. "Get up, now."

With a shudder, he rises to his feet. "Simka...?"

"Take off your clothes." I channel all my frustration and need into the words. "*All* of them this time."

His expression is uncertain. Then, uneasily, he takes off the cloak I gave him, dropping it to the floor. His corporal's jacket follows, but when he reaches his shirt, he pauses.

"Everything," I say. "Now." My desire has erupted into a bonfire, and I can't deny it any longer, not with him standing in this tent with me. I know he feels it, too, but he's too caught up in the lies he's been telling himself to see.

Eyebrows furrowed, Jar'kel obeys, peeling off his shirt to reveal the body I've thought about for so many nights and days, the scarred chest I imagined earlier while I touched myself, wishing it was him, trying desperately to recapture the glorious pleasure he gave me. He unlaces his pants hastily, fumbling to get them off and peel them down his legs.

At last, I see it: the dark blue cock hanging between his thighs. I drop the blanket I've been holding around my naked body, and somehow his eyes get even bigger.

"Get on the bed," I bark. Frozen to the spot, Jar'kel doesn't move until I gesture at the messy pile of furs. "Go."

He follows my instructions, sitting down on the edge of the bed. I climb on top of him, and he gasps as I settle on his lap, that length pressed between my legs as it starts to thicken and swell. Just the sight of it has sent my blood cascading into my hips, filling me with a blistering, carnal desire.

I've needed him so badly, and I know he's needed me, too, by the way his body instantly reacts to mine, hardening for me, his belly tensing and his breaths quickening. I slide along him, dragging my wet heat over the shaft of his cock, and he groans.

"Simka—" he says, but I take his long tusk in my hand and yank his head closer, silencing him.

"Shut up." Before I can take his mouth in mine, though, Jar'kel is already kissing me, seizing me by the nape of my neck and pulling me against him. Our lips crash together, and oh, how I missed his kiss, how it lights me on fire. He groans as I demand he open his mouth for me, my tongue lancing inside to snatch up his. His hands drag down my back, squeezing my flesh, bringing me even closer to his body. He cups my ass in his palms and guides me over his cock again and again, leaving my wetness all along it. His hips jerk with each pass while he consumes me with his lips and tongue and teeth.

I know where he fits, where he belongs. I lift myself up and reach down to find that creature between his legs, taking it roughly in my hands. He groans as I stroke him harshly, pulling the skin up over the wide, mushroom head and then pulling it away again. He's already leaking creamy white from the slit at the tip, and while I may not know much about cocks, I'm pretty sure that means he's starving for me the way I am for him.

"Tell me what it is you really want, Jar'kel," I growl, moving my hand faster. "Without fear. Without trying to do what's best for me. Tell me what you need."

"You," he says without hesitation, his body responding to me with every stroke. "I need *you*."

I position myself so I'm hovering over his waist, the shaft of his cock now resting between us. His eyes are soft but hungry, tender but filled with fear. "Simka, you—"

"I want you to fuck me," I interrupt, sliding myself forward so that thick, heavy thing eases into the divot between my legs, towards that starving spot that will only be sated by him. I rub it across my clit and back again, smearing his juices all over me.

My troll's chest is heaving, his hands trembling even as they clutch me tight against him. His red eyes are as full of lust as they are trepidation. "We won't be able to go back if we do this."

How do I make him see? How do I convince him that I'm not some delicate doll he has to worry about breaking? That huge cockhead slides around my entrance, and Jar'kel groans as his crown presses against my pussy. I need him inside me more than I need food or water or sunshine. I lower myself, fitting that head against the small cavern inside me.

"Stop thinking," I tell him. "And let yourself be happy."

At last, his wall crumbles in front of me. Jar'kel leans down so his forehead rests against mine, and his gravelly voice comes out barely a whisper. "If I am what you want," he says, "then you can have me."

With those words, I let myself sink down, because I know exactly what I want. But that wide cockhead is far, far too big to fit. So I press down harder, and I can't help the cry that comes out of me as everything pinches. My body tries desperately to stretch, but there's so little give.

Jar'kel whimpers my name as I try again. He cradles my body

tight against his, supporting me as I push harder. "Simka, be careful—"

Then something breaks, flooding me with pain, and his cock slips through.

"Ah!" I wasn't prepared for just how much it would hurt. Jar'kel's brows tilt with worry, but as he fills me up so full I think I might just explode, his mouth drops open and a moan escapes his lips. Tears fall from my eyes as that massive girth seeks to fit into my small body. Every part of me is stretching, expanding, trying desperately to accommodate him. Underneath the sharp, blistering pain is a deep satisfaction, a powerful flame of pleasure.

He's right where I need him—right where he belongs.

"Fuck," Jar'kel groans, his face pressing into my shoulder, his tusk cold against my skin. "Simka, I... You feel..."

I try my hardest to fall into his lap, and my troll moans raggedly as I take as much of him into me as I can. Then I rise up again, needing more friction, needing to relive that first thrust with a second one. I slide down over him once more, and the burn returns. Jar'kel's arms wrap around me tight, and he brings his face down to mine, kissing my mouth, my nose, my cheeks. He licks up my tears, then presses his lips to my closed eyes, too. His hands cup my ass, lifting me up, then bringing me gently down over him again. I cry out, my channel spreading wide to fit him, and Jar'kel groans with pleasure. Again, I swallow him up, his cock inside me making a wet sound as it buries itself deep.

"Simka. Simka." He chants my name, wrapping me up as tight as he can in his arms, his tusks framing my face as he plunders my mouth. I continue lifting my hips and then lowering them, reuniting with him over and over again. Every time we come together, a bolt of searing bliss lances through me. It's as if I can feel his pleasure inside me, seeping in through his flesh against mine as my pussy wraps around him tight. It throbs with both pain and bliss.

"It hurts, doesn't it?" he says quietly, slowing my movements.

I bite my lip and nod, because I can't lie to him, not ever again. He slowly eases me up, so his cock slips out of me.

"Jar'kel," I whimper, because I need him back. He kisses me roughly, letting me know just how much he wants me. Curling his arms around my body, he switches our positions so I'm now down on the bed, my belly exposed to him.

He crouches over me, a huge, blue beast, his lips twisted up with pure hunger as he spreads my legs. Fisting the root of his cock in his hand, he guides it once more between my legs.

"I'm going to fill you so full of me," he says, panting, a feverish desperation in his eyes I've never seen before. "I'm going to fuck you until you drench my cock."

Just his words send fire spreading across my body. "Yes," I whine. "Yes, please!"

When he enters me from this position, he slides in as smooth as silk. I cry out, and he grips my thighs so tight that his nails bite into my skin. It hurts much less like this, and as he buries himself deep, all I feel is him.

This is the Jar'kel who's been waiting inside, held in tight so he doesn't devour me. Now I want to be consumed.

My troll pulls out, gasping for air, his red eyes huge and soft and yet ravenous. His way is even easier now, even slicker, as he pumps in and out, his hips thrusting wildly as he takes me. He falls down onto his elbows and presses another kiss to my lips, sliding his tongue through them, worrying them in his teeth. I don't realize that I'm calling out his name over and over as he fills me and then empties me again, his cock dragging over a blistering-hot place inside me.

Now, I can see all of him. Jar'kel's tough defenses have peeled away, and in its place is a tender soul that aches for connection. I want to wrap my hands around it and hold it softly, to tell it he will never be alone again, not while I live. He is mine, thoroughly, completely, and I am his. The bright line that links us together is now unbreakable.

Jar'kel reaches down between us, where our bodies are joined, and strokes my spread lips. Then he glances over my clit with his thumb, and my whole body jerks under him as pure euphoria ripples through me. Again and again, he thrusts while rubbing me, his own moans matching mine. Through the ache, a powerful pleasure is spreading across my body, tendrils of fire racing through my skin. My head falls back and I'm screaming now, my neck taut with all of my unspent tension. My thighs wrap tight around his hips, drawing him deeper, and Jar'kel moans helplessly as his hand moves even faster.

"Fuck, Simka!" His shoulders curl tight to protect us, to shield us from the world. Together we are a barrier against the storm, holding it up as one. "You are mine. *Mine.* Forever." He gasps the words as he pumps harder, that hand drawing me tighter and tighter around him, until he's struggling to pull his cock out again. His red eyes are locked on mine as he plunders me, and I know then that he feels what I do, how we're now twined together, two parts of one.

"I am," I moan. "Forever." I don't know how long forever will be, but I'll treasure all of it.

The sensation creeping up my neck is unlike anything I've ever felt before. My whole body goes rigid, my muscles screaming for relief as finally, I go sprinting right off the edge of my peak. I sob my pleasure as I tumble over into nothingness, clinging to Jar'kel with all of my pent-up hopes and dreams. He tries to pull out of me, but I'm clenched so tight around him he struggles to move.

"You're so tight," he groans. "Yes. Give me everything." He thrusts in once more, harder and deeper than ever before, and a burst of wet heat fills me up. Jar'kel crushes me under him as he pumps again, and again, filling me up even more, slamming into me with all the power in his body, his cock making obscene sounds as his come spurts out.

Finally, his frantic motions stop, and he collapses. My troll brackets my face with his one whole tusk and his one broken one, and we're panting as if we've both run ten miles.

"My Simka," Jar'kel whispers as his torrent leaks out of me, running down to my ass. Now the bite is more exquisite than ever, but instead I float along on the slowly-receding wave of my pleasure. He draws me close to him, squeezing me so tight I might vanish into him.

"My Jar'kel," I whisper back, and he chuckles against my forehead, kissing it over and over.

At last, I'm where I belong.

Chapter 18

Jar'kel

I can't deny it. Simka is everything, the culmination of my whole long life, of every hardship and struggle, and even the small victories. She's my missing piece, my other half. I can sense her heart, fiery and free, inside mine as she sews up all my damaged edges, knitting them neatly back together. When I roll over, my cock still buried inside her, a pained mewl tumbles out of her mouth, and I kiss it away. Then, slowly, I withdraw, spilling my seed all over the furs.

As hard as I try not to think about what it might do inside her, I can't help the pride that sweeps through me. What if I do plant a whelp in my Simka? My cock twitches at the idea of my wild, round-faced woman in her fur coat, swelled up with me, her perfect, round breasts leaking milk while I suck on them. I think of my former lieutenant, walking around the marketplace with his orc daughter on his shoulders, and I wonder if our whelp will come out looking like me or like her.

I crush her tight against me and draw the furs up over us, twining our legs together. She settles into the crook of my shoulder, still drawing heavy, gasping breaths. I imagine the rest of our lives, my cock sliding in and out of her, and already I want her again. The weeks of holding it all in have built up into a storm, but her small, soft body will need time to recover.

I want to say something, to sweep away all the resentment and fear between us, but when I look down, I find Simka is already asleep. So I lean my head against hers, angling my face so I don't spear her with my good tusk, and let my eyes fall closed.

For the first time in my life, I feel peace.

Night has fallen by the time I wake up. Strangely, my arms are empty, and a wave of panic washes over me.

My mate. Where did she go? I sit up, panting, wondering if she's changed her mind and left me.

Then the tent flap opens and Simka steps inside, carrying our dinner. "It's cold," she says, "but Vavi saved us some." She sets it on the table and returns to the bed, peeling the furs back to climb in next to me. She winces as she adjusts her legs, and I draw a hand down her cheek. The world around us dissipates until she's all I can see.

I want to tell her what she means to me, how I've spent my whole life looking for her, but I don't want to press her. This truce between us is fragile. I'll have to work hard to earn back her trust, but I will succeed. I'll spend the rest of my life showing her what she means to me, how she's the only reason I still exist. I nuzzle my face in her hair, filling up my nose with the perfect smell of her.

Once I'm certain Simka is asleep again, I bundle her up tight in the furs and climb out of bed. Some air will do me good. I snatch a few pieces of cold food off the plate before shrugging on my jacket and cloak and heading out into the night.

Torches are lit around the camp, and for the first time, I can pick out the fresh smell of the snow, the whisper of the cold, starry sky, and the tang of burning wood. Everything feels new, as if I'm a whelp again myself.

I stand there, breathing in the frigid air, my eyes closed—until a voice startles me.

"Good to see you up and about, corporal." Gorren wears a huge smirk, and I know then that the entire camp heard us fucking earlier. Simka was not quiet, and I have my doubts she ever will be. No, not my mountain woman. She will tell the entire world when I pleasure her, and I relish the thought.

I cross my arms. "Once you're done being smug, tell me what you want."

He laughs heartily. "Well, in a day or two I want to see you in my tent. We have a lot to talk about. But until then..." He points off in the direction of the peak. "The hot spring. You should take her there."

"Hot spring?" I ask.

"There's a cave that leads into the mountain, and inside is a hot spring. It's a good place to mend your bond."

That means leaving the camp. I quirk an eyebrow at this bold suggestion.

"I trust you won't leave now," Gorren says, and I want to wipe that knowing grin right off his face. "I'll have one of the guards show you the way."

With that, he waves at me and departs for the leader's tent.

I know I can't return to my post in Morgenzan, among the city guard—not with a human mate of my own. I watched how society treated my captain and my lieutenant when they took the leap to be together, and I don't want that for Simka. She deserves to be accepted, to be free to live her life, and this may be the only place in this whole idiotic world we can possibly do that.

If I want Simka at my side, and still keep my head, I really have no choice but to give the orcs what they want.

SIMKA

For the first time in what feels like months, I sleep thoroughly and soundly, curled up with my troll. With my Jar'kel.

Already it seems the lines on his face have lessened, as if whole years were wiped off his slate. When he suggests we go to the hot spring the next morning, I'm skeptical that we'll be allowed to leave the camp.

"It was Gorren's idea," he says with a shrug. "It will probably help with the pain."

I can't deny how tender I feel between the legs, so we bundle up and leave with one of the guards in the direction of the mountain. There's a tall wood panel propped in the opening of a cave, which he pulls aside for us. Once we pass through, he hands us a torch, then closes it again behind us and takes up his post outside.

So Gorren doesn't quite trust us not to leave. I don't blame him.

The moist heat of the springs descends on us the moment we step inside the cave. Jar'kel lights the torches along the wall as we pass, and the tunnel is long and winding, the shape of it strangely, perfectly round, like some enormous snake burrowed through the rock.

As we press deeper, a shimmer of purple light appears up ahead. What could that be? Jar'kel looks just as surprised as I am as we round a bend, and the glow grows even brighter. He takes my hand and tucks it in his palm, keeping me close.

Then the tunnel gives way, sprawling outward into a wide cavern. The ceiling rises high above us, as if the whole mountain is hollow. The air is humid and warm, but what really draws my eyes are the carvings all across the walls. The grooves are filled with an ethereal, purple brilliance.

"What is this?" I breathe, following the carvings around the cave. Drawn on each side are a pair of faces, one clearly trollkin, with great curving tusks, sitting nose-to-nose with a human face, which is flatter and softer. Beneath the faces, their hands are clasped together. The entire image is glowing.

"Magic." Jar'kel is just as wide-eyed as I am. "It looks just like the magic Gorren showed me." We walk together to one of the walls, where he draws his finger along the image.

"Should you really be touching it?" I ask, skeptical.

"I think it's safe." His finger comes away a little dusty, but that's all. "This must be where it came from." We both gaze upward, where swirls of purple continue to the domed ceiling of the cavern.

"I don't understand." I back away from the wall, still holding Jar'kel's hand. "Why is this here? I feel like it... means something."

He nods in agreement. "This place must be how the wild orcs learned about human mates." He looks troubled. "It's ancient. The tunnel that brought us here?" I nod. "Surely left behind by one of the great worms."

I'm only vaguely familiar with the stories. Once upon a time, our world was occupied by monstrous creatures, and it was far more dangerous for humans and trollkin alike. But over time the beasts died out, allowing us to spread across the world, and eventually turn on one another.

"Whoever carved these drawings must have found the tunnels, and then hid this here," I say. I feel brave enough to touch the markings myself, but nothing happens. "Why?"

Jar'kel simply shakes his head. "I don't know for sure, but if what Gorren says is true... they must have hidden it here for safe-keeping. And the clan is trying to continue that work."

Neither of us has any more answers than that, so at last we turn to the springs at the far end of the cavern. They're steaming, and fed by water trickling down a set of tiered pools. The scent of sulfur rises from the surface as we walk up to them hand-in-hand.

I'm about to strip down when Jar'kel steps behind me, wrapping his arms around my waist. He tugs the cord of my cloak loose, bringing it down from my shoulders. I fall still as he takes the rest of my clothes off, slowly, intentionally. Then his own follow, until we're both naked in front of each other. Without the feverish heat of our first time together rushing through my blood, I can finally appreciate all of him.

He's been carved by time, the same as this cave, into something beautiful. I reach up to his face, smoothing out his crow's feet, and he closes his eyes as I trace down his cheeks to the lines around his mouth. I continue my exploration with the pads of my fingers, over his broad shoulders to his chest, past long lines of puckered skin. I want to know the story behind every single scar, but for now, I don't want to say a word—I just want to feel him.

I kneel down as I draw my hands over Jar'kel's hips, tracing the curved line of muscle from his hip to his groin. His cock is already starting to awaken for me, but I ignore it as I pass further southward, over his thick thighs to his rounded calves, all the way to his feet and four toes. The skin is thick as leather from walking barefoot as he did before coming here, to the far north. My troll is growing harder for me, and his breaths are less even as my hand wanders up the inside of his thigh to the dark blue sac hanging between his legs. I brush over it with my fingers, and he exhales a sharp breath of air.

I remember what he did for me, how his tongue felt between my legs, and make a decision. Taking his cock in my hand, it instantly surges to life and Jar'kel tries to hold in his groan.

"Let me hear you," I murmur, and he twitches in my hand at the command. First I stroke him, bringing that swollen thing fully to life in my palms, before I put my mouth on it.

At this he moans, and it's a full-throated sound, as I asked. I lick up the salty fluid that's already begun dripping from it, and I love how it tastes of *him*. Next, I tease with my tongue, to test how he reacts, and it seems to please him immensely. I cage my lips around the head, experimenting further, and his hips jerk, his hand resting on my hair.

I wonder what else I can do. When I bring even more of him into my mouth, Jar'kel mutters, "Fuck, Simka," like a prayer. "You're incredible."

If he likes this, then I'll do even more. I swallow his cock deeper and deeper, until it's as far back in my throat as it can go without choking me. I reach around behind him as I pump my mouth over him, exploring the dense muscle of his ass, and squeeze it tight as I emulate as best I can what it might feel like to be inside me. He groans even louder.

I want to suck him in more, but I've reached my limit. How did this thing fit inside me? Wrapping my hand around the root of his cock, I stroke in time with my lips, and his gasps speed up. I sample his balls with my other hand, rolling them about as I learn them better.

"Shit," he moans, his head falling back. "Simka, I'm going to shoot off into your mouth."

"Good," I try to say, but the word comes out garbled as I take him deeper. I stroke faster and suck harder, and Jar'kel's voice rises in pitch until suddenly he tenses all over, and I pump even more vigorously until hot, salty seed pours out, hitting my tongue. I try to swallow as much as I can, but it's too much, and it slips down my chin. I pull away, coughing.

Jar'kel chuckles breathlessly, and kneels down in front of me.

He takes my face in his hands and kisses me, licking himself off me, which is so sexy and filthy that warmth pools in my belly.

"Next time," he whispers, "I want it inside you." I shiver at the thought as he helps me back up to my feet. Never letting go of my hand, he leads me toward the spring, and sweeps me up into his arms before climbing in.

Chapter 19

Jar'kel

She is a true wonder, taking me into her mouth that way. If I hadn't been her first time under the blankets myself, I wouldn't believe she'd never done it before. But I can already sense her body tuned in to mine, speaking the same language, so I'm also not surprised.

I hold Simka in my lap as I find a place to rest in the spring. It's the perfect temperature, just hot enough that it doesn't burn. My human gasps as her lower body slips under the warm water, and her eyes clench closed in pain. I rub up and down her thighs, over her belly, wishing I could touch her down below the water but knowing she's far too raw. Along the edge of the rock spring are a variety of soaps, and I scoot along the stone to grab one.

In silence I clean my mate's body, every inch of it. She steadily relaxes into my arms, and her head drifts to my bicep with a satisfied sigh. I worship her, relishing the soft give of her under my hands, the way her chest rises into my touch as I brush over her nipples. I can't help leaning down to suck on them, and her moan fills me with the deepest pleasure possible. As troubling as it is to imagine putting a whelp in this small woman, and what that means for the future... I also crave it in my soul. I palm each of her small, pert breasts, then smooth my hand over her belly, my cock rising again as I picture her as ripe and round as her sister is now. She giggles as it pokes into her back.

"Already?" she asks, eyes twinkling. "My jaw is a little sore. You'll have to wait."

I can't help but laugh. She is mischievous but also honest, my Simka. I've longed for her my whole life and never even knew it.

Then it's my turn. She cleans me all over, even running her soapy hand down my ass, between my cheeks. This piques her interest, and she explores the puckered hole there with her finger. My mate's curiosity about my body is limitless.

"Maybe another time," I tell her, and she nods quickly before moving on. I can't wait to explore every bodily pleasure with her.

When she's finished, I take her into my lap again and lean back in the water, drawing her against my chest. We lie like that in silence, listening to the gentle sound of the spring flowing in. Occasionally I scoop up hot water and drizzle it down her chest, between her breasts, and she curls up against me closer.

Is this what happiness feels like? I could simply drift away into it, the warmth and pleasure of bathing with my mate.

"I want to go back."

Simka's voice startles me out of my doze. I blink a few times. "Go back where?" I ask.

Her eyes drop down to her lap. "Home."

My heart sinks. Gorren will never let her go back to her village. And even if he did... I doubt her family would accept me. Not an ugly old troll.

I sit up and embrace her, locking my arms tight around her. "You can't. You know Gorren won't let you, and if we escape..." I kiss her collar bone, then nuzzle it with my nose while I hold her tight. "This can't exist out there."

Simka kicks the water, sending it splashing. "But I have to. My dad needs to know I'm all right. I can't let him wonder forever."

What is it like to have a parent, to have that bond with a family member? If I'm honest, I'm a little envious.

"I'm sorry." That's all I can think to say. Unless we plan to sneak away like we'd once wanted to, she'll never get to see home again. And out there, there's no future for us.

Simka turns her head, burying her face in my armpit. There she stays, silent, until we're both wrinkled from head to toe and much too hot. She still doesn't speak as we climb out and sit on the edge of the spring to let our bodies dry. It's not as cold as I would expect, being inside a frigid mountain at this altitude, but it's like some supernatural power is keeping it warm.

I'm being selfish, I know. I want to stay because here, maybe I can keep her close to me. But Simka can't be trapped. She longs for freedom and independence.

As I stroke her short hair, my resolve clicks into place.

"If leaving here is truly what you want, more than anything..." I take a deep breath. "Then of course I'll help you."

She tilts her face up to mine, eyes bright. "You will?"

I would do anything for her. The realization is both my deepest and most terrifying truth.

I nod. "We'll find a way to get you home."

SIMKA

With Jar'kel at my side, I feel braver than ever. He is clever and wise, and I am stubborn and determined. Whatever obstacles are in our way, I'm confident we can conquer them together.

That night, Jar'kel takes off my clothes and lays me back on the bed, trailing his hands down my body until he reaches the crux of my thighs. There he licks me, avoiding my tender center until I'm gushing into his mouth. He swallows it all eagerly, and then I do the same for him. When we're both sated, we lie under the furs together, curled up to stay warm.

In the springs, I feel like I finally saw his real, true self, luxuriating in the water and caring for all my small needs. He smiled and played, and it mesmerized me.

I wonder what Dad would think. Will he still accept me? Will he still love me, knowing I won't leave Jar'kel's side?

That unsettling thought follows me into sleep.

The next day, we hatch our plan, keeping our voices low even inside our tent. We pay attention to the guard rotation, and Jar'kel points out the two orcs he met the other night at the bonfire. He's willing to distract them long enough for me to sneak out, even though it would put him at great risk. He still has information, and doesn't believe Gorren would kill him—but he would certainly never be able to leave again.

He would be willing to do that, for me. And I'm just desperate enough to get home. But without a doubt, I would return for him. I would get him out, however I needed to.

But that's not where our trouble ends. Even if I successfully escaped, I would have to get back down the mountain alone, without my ice picks, unless I can find the path the wild orcs take when they attack.

Still, Jar'kel agrees to supply Gorren with some useful nuggets of knowledge so perhaps he can earn the clan leader's trust. If he can find out when the next raid is coming and convince the orcs we won't try to leave, it might just give us an opening. I hope that we can get out of this together.

After a few days, where we sleep curled up tight together at night and spend our days exploring the camp or visiting the hot spring, that gnawing pain between my legs has ebbed. Jar'kel examines me after dinner, and tests me out with one slick finger. But it only feels good, and he gets a satisfied look on his face when I gasp with pleasure.

"I want you," I tell him, running my hand down his lithe body to the dark blue cock between his legs, then wrapping my fingers firmly around it and tugging to show what I need. "Please."

His lip peels up on one side in a mischievous grin that I love. He smiles much more often now.

"Then you'll have it," he says.

Jar'kel keeps me on my back, and kisses me from my throat down between my breasts, cupping them in his palms and squeezing them together. He attends to all of my body, using his four big fingers to tell me how he feels. As he creeps lower, he takes my nipples into his mouth and taunts them with the tips of his teeth, circling them with his tongue.

"These are perfect," he murmurs, plucking each one before moving down my belly, where he swipes my belly button with his tongue, then slicks it down between my legs. There, he teases just my outer lips, and I wriggle to bring him in deeper, to the pearl that craves his attention. Jar'kel gives in, just a fleeting touch over the tip of it, making my hips jolt. He swipes down, covering his fingers in my wetness before returning, using it to slide back and forth over my clit. It earns him a moan from me, and he licks his lips, casting one hungry look up at my face before he leans in and licks.

My body rises up into his mouth, insisting on more. He flicks with his tongue, again and again, while his hand continues to tease my entrance.

"Please," I gasp. "Put it in, please."

Jar'kel chuckles against my pussy and obliges, fitting one of those big fingers inside me. I'm so wet that it glides in, filling me up. I wonder how his cock could possibly fit.

"Open up for me," he croons, burying it deeper. He curls it inside me and rubs along my channel, and the sensation lights a spark of pleasure that ripples outward, making my legs tremble. Soon a second finger prods at me, seeking to slide in, too. I wriggle as it widens me, and after some convincing, my body parts for it. More moans tumble from my lips as he uses both of them to pet my inner walls in long, gentle strokes. I'm already clenching around him, his tongue speeding up as he works inside me, and I think my body might simply come apart.

It feels as if he has a map of me, and knows just where to touch. "Jar'kel," I moan, fisting my hands in his hair. "Your mouth is fucking incredible." I feel him grin against me, then he moves even faster, lavishing affection on my pussy, his fingers hinting at what he'll feel like when our bodies are finally joined again. I find myself at the top of a steep slope, and soon my feet slide out from under me, sending me careening down. My undoing strikes me so hard and so fast that something inside me bursts, and Jar'kel gasps as liquid erupts over his face.

I try to pull away, concerned, but he grabs my ass with his other hand and roots me to the spot.

"What happened?" I ask, panting, my muscles still trembling.

"You gave me a gift," he says, wiping a gratuitous amount of liquid from his face. He licks his lips and closes his eyes, as if savoring it. My cheeks heat as he withdraws his fingers, which are also dripping wet. He kneels down between my legs and covers the head of his cock in my fluids, stroking himself to pull the skin back and expose even more. I watch as he brings himself toward that eager place at the crux of my thighs, and my heart is racing, just imagining being together again. My folds part for him, and Jar'kel drags that soft cockhead up and down along me, across my oversensitive nub and then down again.

"Please," I whimper, arching my back to bring him in closer. "I need it. I need *you.*"

I love the way the lines around his mouth deepen when he smiles. He presses himself into me, gripping his cock hard as if to still it. With a few deep breaths, he looks into my eyes, and there's a tenderness there I never thought I would see—that I never imagined someone would grant me. Behind it I feel as if I can see his whole soul, every soft and sharp edge of it.

Then he pushes in. He's made me so swollen and wet for him that his wide head easily slips through. I cry out as it pauses, just barely inside me, spreading me so wide I marvel that it can even fit. Jar'kel gasps and pitches forward, bracing his arms to either side of me.

"Fuck, Simka," he groans, squeezing his eyes closed. "You feel…" He swallows hard, then ever so slightly pushes in deeper. My head falls back into the furs, and I don't know how my body manages to accommodate him. "You feel so good. Better than any cunt in the entire world."

He remains shallow, giving me only a sip of what he'll feel like fully seated in me, and I whimper and moan, my body strained by what he's given me already and yet begging for more.

"Give it to me," I whimper, gripping his shoulders tight. "All of it, Jar'kel."

After a few more teasing strokes, my troll obliges at last, his powerful hips thrusting the rest of the way in. I sob his name as he finds his place deep inside me, and I'm so full, so stretched that I can't fathom taking any more. I moan as I welcome him completely. My walls wrap tight around him, and Jar'kel grunts, sweat beading on his forehead.

"You take my cock so perfectly," he whispers, leaning down to touch his nose to mine, his tusks scraping my cheeks.

I close my eyes and rest my forehead against his. "I was made to fit you."

He exhales a long, deep breath, and then his eyes twinkle. "Just as I was made to fuck you."

Jar'kel takes me slowly, sipping my nipples, kissing my lips as he strokes in and out. When I'm slick and moaning, he sits back, watching where his cock is filling me.

"You're beautiful, Simka," he tells me, slowing to slide his fingers along my spread lower lips, as if marveling at how our bodies so neatly complement one another. "Flawless."

Of course I love all of his compliments, but I need more of him, too, so I curl my legs around his waist, urging him to take me. I crave all of him, his mind and his body and his soul. Jar'kel's expression turns feral as he crouches over me, clutching my ass tight as he hastens his strokes. Now he's filling me as full as he can and then sliding out, over and over. Desperate to be closer, to feel his pounding heart against mine, I curl a hand around his tusk and drag him down so I can look in his eyes. There, I can see him, all of him, and it's bewitching.

His arms draw me in, pressing my breasts to his bare chest as he tests every angle, listening as I reward him with my cries. He finds my most tender place and tilts his hips to strike it, again and again, and I relish the flexing of his abdomen as he fills me up and empties me, until he's as lost to his pleasure as I am.

"Damn," he growls, clenching his eyes shut. He pauses, breathing hard, his arms trembling. "You're so tight. I can barely —" He interrupts himself with a groan, and he clenches me tight against him as he bursts inside me. Gasping, he falls down, keeping from crushing me with one elbow. His eyes are wide and surprised. "You felt so good, I couldn't stop it." I get the sense from his tone of voice that it's been a long time since that happened to him.

I grin and caress his cheek. "Guess you'll have to do it again."

At my words, his still-hard cock twitches inside me, and he leans his head into the curve of my throat. Soon he's moving again, an obscene, wet sound following every thrust of his hips as his own wetness eases his way. Jar'kel abruptly pulls back, and I whimper when his cock slides free of me—but he's not done. He flips me onto my hands and knees with ease.

"There we are," he says into my ear, pressing his wet cock between the cheeks of my ass. "Now I can see even more of you."

Gripping me tight, he slides his cock in again, filling me more than ever in this position. I cry out and instinctually rock back against him, taking him deeper, and deeper, his hot come dripping down over my clit with every pump of his hips.

It's not long before the sensation of his cockhead dragging over all my creases and folds leads me to my breaking point. Color bursts in front of my eyes, and I sob out his name as I convulse around him. Jarkel lets out a breathless moan, thrusting through it, fucking me harder, giving me a firm slap to the ass as he continues plundering me. Bent over me, he whispers in my ear.

"You're going to get so big with my whelp," he murmurs, his tusk tangling in my hair. "I'm going to put so many of them inside you."

I think of all his dripping seed finding purchase in my womb, and as his cock swells up fat inside me, I easily meet my roaring pleasure once again. Here, his soul tastes sweet, open and waiting for me to be one with him. Inside he is playful, and hungering for a family, for happiness.

Jar'kel groans as he shoves himself as far in as he can, and erupts. He crouches over me, panting, stroking my ass and then squeezing it.

I want nothing else but my troll, as long as I live.

CHAPTER 20

JAR'KEL

How my little Simka's cunt clenches me so tight, how her cries fill the air, how her body trembles as I fill her up—there is nothing like it, nothing like *her*.

I withdraw slowly, cupping one hand over her pink, swollen slit as my seed drips out. She collapses to the bed, and I draw my hands down her thighs, kneading the tight muscle with my fingers. Boneless, my human lies there as I attend to her, smoothing over her trembling calves and her firm butt. She shudders under me, and I'm amazed at how much my cock already longs to be inside her once more. I assure it that we will have her again and again, until her breasts are full of milk and she's ripe with my whelp.

Simka's eyes are closed when I lie down next to her, heavy breaths still falling from her lips. She moans as she rolls over to face me, and without hesitation she curls against my body, her sweet arms wrapping around my waist. I trace the swell of her hip, and lean down to whisper to her.

"You are a marvel." I draw her in closer, relishing the feel of her warm body and heaving chest.

"You're very good at that," she says into my skin, nuzzling me. "I don't like to think about how you learned."

I quirk an eyebrow. Is she jealous of an unnamed, unknown woman? I think of Pa'zi and almost laugh, because nothing I shared with her compares to being with my Simka, but I think this feisty human would be quite insulted if I laughed.

"It has never been this way with anyone," I assure her, stroking her hair. "I understand your body without being told, and I believe it understands me."

She nods vigorously. "Oh, you certainly speak its language."

Now I do chuckle, immensely gratified at having made her second time pleasurable. I look forward to exploring even more bodily joys with her, from now until...

I shake my head to keep the thought away. We have much more time ahead of us. I can't fear looking down the barrel of a gun that isn't even loaded yet.

Still, as Simka drifts off in my arms, I hope that I can have many, many more years with her.

In the following days, I spend most of my afternoons in Gorren's tent, sharing what information I feel is safe to share—just enough to be useful to him, but not so much that he would be capable of taking the whole city of Morgenzan in a night raid. Many of the city guard are blameless in this, simply doing their duty to the city and those who lord over it. Soon he asks my opinion on potential moves, and I think he's beginning to trust me.

At night, I luxuriate in Simka's body and her powerful, sturdy heart. She loves to ride my face, and more than once she's had to clean my seed off of her small, round tits. Sometimes I tell her what to do, but more often she's the one who leads me to what she wants. My woman has no trouble telling me how to fuck her.

We take notes of the guard patterns, who is on which shifts. During the day, Simka helps around the camp to make herself indispensable, and at night we join in the revelry. When the ale flows and the wild orcs fuck beside the fire, she drags me away to our tent so she can have me in private.

At last, Gorren tells me when they're going on their next raid —in just a few days' time. They're aiming to strike at dawn, right at the shift change. It's the perfect opportunity for Simka to escape. I can distract the guards with some lighthearted conversation while she slips away and searches for the path down the mountain.

I won't be able to go with her, but at least she'll be able to see her father again. Gorren will likely let me live, if I still have more intelligence to give him. Simka promises she'll find a way back, a way to get me out of here safely, but I don't count on it.

I've never been one to sacrifice myself for others, but for her, I would do anything.

We are only days away from executing our plan when Vavi's screams fill the camp.

They are not the screams of pleasure, but of agony. Simka gets up so fast she spills her food, and rushes out of the tent. I'm close behind, and we're not the only ones. Other orcs peer out, and an orcess sprints past us as we hurry toward the sound of Vavi's wails. Simka follows, panic written across her face.

She throws open the flap of the leader's tent, and instantly recoils.

Blood. Vavi is moaning in pain where she lies on their bed, blood pooling around her legs. Gorren kneels beside her, his eyes filled with abject terror when he turns to look at us. Already the orcess is between Vavi's thighs as she lets out another miserable cry.

"It's too soon," the orcess says in Trollkin, brow furrowed. "Too soon." Vavi wriggles to get away as the orcess examines her, and her face is pale.

"My baby," Vavi mutters, clutching her belly. "Please." Simka takes her hand and squeezes it, kneeling beside Gorren.

After her brief examination, the orcess pulls away and shakes her head. "I don't know what I can do to help except ease the pain," she tells the clan leader in Trollkin. "She is human. Perhaps the whelp isn't—"

"No," Gorren snarls, rising to his feet. He towers over her, and the orcess shrinks back. "You have to help her."

She holds up her hands. "I can't. I don't have the knowledge. And if the blood doesn't stop... she's going to die."

Simka's shoulders tremble, and I crouch down behind her, smoothing my hands down her arms.

"This isn't right," she says, clutching Vavi's hand as her sister sobs again. "This shouldn't be happening."

"I've seen a human carry whelps before," I say. "It was difficult, but she survived. Something else must be wrong."

Abruptly Simka rises to her feet, and glares up at Gorren. "We have to take her home." Her voice is hard and firm. "There's a healer and a midwife in my village. That might be her only chance."

"No!" Gorren's words are sharp and final. Simka doesn't need to understand his language to know what he's saying. "She does not leave my sight!"

I step between them. "Then I'll go fetch the midwife and bring her here," I say.

"They cannot know where we are." Gorren clenches his hand into a fist, but it's still shaking.

"Then she'll die." He turns his deadly glare on me, but he

doesn't intimidate me. "And there's nothing you can do for her here."

"If we go to the human village, we'll be killed." The orc falls back to his knees at her side. "The city guard will surely come for us."

I translate for Simka, because Gorren is too far out of his mind to speak her tongue.

"Then let us help her!" She's frantic. "Please. Let me save my sister and take her home."

I rest a hand on Gorren's shoulder. "Tell us how to get down the mountain," I say calmly, "and we'll take her to the village, where she might have a chance of surviving this. Do you truly want to lose her?"

Slowly, the defiance drains from his face as he realizes he has no other choice. This is the only path that doesn't reveal the location of the camp.

Gorren gets to his feet, his eyes ringed with red, and turns to me. "I'm trusting you, troll," he snarls. "She will live, or you will be a corpse."

I nod. I understand his pain, now that I have Simka. If it were her lying in her own blood, I'd be angry and delirious, too.

"I'll make sure she gets there safely." I jerk my head at Simka. "We're taking Vavi," I say in Freysian. "Help her up so I can carry her."

"All the way down the mountain?" Simka asks, aghast.

I nod. "All the way down the mountain."

Vavi cries out as we help her upright, and I lift her into my arms. Blood drips from her legs, streaming over my hands. Simka leaps to her feet and leads me out of the tent.

"That way," Gorren says in a shaking voice, and points to the south end of camp. "Over the ridge, there is a narrow pathway that leads down the mountain. The village will be due east." He takes Vavi's hand in his and kisses it desperately.

"Please don't send me away," Vavi moans, clutching his hand tight. "Please, Gorren! My father won't let me come back to you."

"But you live." He offers her a pained smile. "And I will find you again. Go with them."

Vavi hiccups as I carry her off, a guard accompanying us. Gorren falls down to his knees, dropping his head in his hands, as we leave him behind.

SIMKA

My sister is dying. I can feel it in my own veins. Now we know the way home, but we've learned this information at an incredible cost.

Jar'kel doesn't struggle at all to carry Vavi, even as we make our way down the steep pathway in our snowshoes. We leave a trail of red behind us as my sister continues to moan in pain, but she's lost so much blood that she grows quieter with every passing minute. I can only hope we get her home in time to save her life.

"Hurry," I beg Jar'kel, even though we're moving as fast as we can. He simply nods and picks up his pace. Sweat courses down his forehead, but he's strong and I know he can carry her to the village, as long as she survives until then.

The path is treacherous and winding, but it's passable. The sun is getting low in the sky by the time we reach the base of the mountain. I recognize where we are—quite far from where I was searching before. I would never have guessed to go this way, and chastise myself for how many months I wasted looking in the wrong place.

"Follow me," I tell him, and we head off into the dense ever-green trees toward home. Vavi has stopped making any sound.

When I push the hair away from her face, her eyes open halfway. She smiles a weak, eerie smile.

"Simka," she whispers. "It's you." She says it as if we haven't been living in the same camp together for the last few weeks.

Jar'kel and I move even faster, though both of us are utterly exhausted. But when the village appears up ahead of us, I find a new well of strength and take off running towards it.

"Help!" I call out, sprinting through the village gate. "Someone help! Call Masha!" I barrel past house after house, calling out my request.

"Simka?" It's my father's voice. He drops the armful of logs he's carrying and rushes towards me, tears already pouring down his face. "Simka!" He pulls me into his arms, squeezing me tight. "Where have you been?"

"There's no time, Dad," I say, trying to wriggle away. "Vavi's dying."

He releases me, blinking. "Vavi's alive?"

That's when Jar'kel appears, carrying my sister, covered in her blood. My father's eyes narrow, and he reaches for the axe hanging off his belt.

"No!" I grab his arm to stop him. "Jar'kel carried her all this way from the orc camp. Please, go get Masha. Vavi's going to die if we don't help her."

I can tell he's torn between his rage and my command, but finally, he dips his head and takes off running into the row of houses, calling out Masha's name. Other villagers have gathered, whispering and pointing but not coming near us. I lead Jar'kel toward our own home and nearly kick down the door. Inside, we find the bed where Vavi slept for her whole childhood, and he gingerly lays her down on it.

Vavi's eyes flutter open as Dad rushes back into the house. Jar'kel steps out of the room to make room for Masha, the village midwife, to come inside.

Vavi smiles faintly. "Dad." He grabs her hand and squeezes it. His eyes finally take in her big belly, and he glares at me with unfathomable fury.

"What's happened?" he demands, getting to his feet as Masha begins her examination. He drags me out of the room, where Jar'kel stands drenched in blood. "And you!" He looks ready to cleave my troll in half.

"Now's not the time, Dad," I hiss. "It wasn't my choice not to come back. I've been—"

"She's wanted to return to you for weeks," Jar'kel says in his deep baritone. "But we've been prisoners. It was outside her control."

Dad's face falls, and he suddenly grabs me with both arms, hugging me for everything I'm worth. I wanted to come back home so badly, to see my father and hug him again, but not like this.

"Please don't ever lie to me again," he says, squeezing me tighter.

In the other room, we hear Vavi cry out, and together we rush back inside.

Masha is getting to her feet. "We have to get this baby out," she says, giving all of us stern looks. "That's the only way she'll live."

"Do whatever you have to do to save my daughter." Dad grips my shoulder hard.

Masha nods in understanding and runs from the house. I retrieve a cloth and dip it in cold water, running it over Vavi's forehead until the midwife returns, carrying a large bag of equipment. Masha hastily mixes up a solution and pours it down Vavi's throat, who then chokes on it. Then, bringing out a pair of great big tongs, the midwife kneels down at the base of the bed and spreads Vavi's legs apart.

My poor sister moans in agony as Masha reaches inside with her tool, and I clutch my sister's hand in mine. She squeezes as hard as she can, but she has very little strength left. I rub her forehead with the cool cloth while she's hit by another wave of pain.

"Push really hard," Masha instructs. Vavi sobs, and before I realize it, I'm sobbing, too.

A strong hand lands on my shoulder. Jar'kel is standing behind me, lending me his strength. He strokes my hair, and whispers in my ear.

"She will survive, I know it. And so will the whelp."

I have no choice but to hope he's right.

As Masha pulls, Vavi lets out a horrible, agonized scream. Dad is beside us, smoothing back her sweat-soaked hair.

"Get out of here, troll," he snarls at Jar'kel. "You have no place in this room."

With a brief nod, Jar'kel kisses my head and leaves. I don't have the fortitude to argue.

Vavi's sobs echo through the house as Masha pulls harder. More blood pours across the bed. My own tears are an ocean as I watch my sister die in front of me. Misery and fury mix into terrible outrage. If Gorren hadn't trapped us in that miserable camp, none of this would have happened.

And then... a sharp cry fills the air. Masha gasps as she pulls the infant free, and Vavi lets out a miserable moan. Hurriedly the midwife hands me the baby, covered in blood, and returns to her place between Vavi's legs. She mixes up a paste and applies it, trying desperately to staunch the flow.

"Let me see," my sister says weakly. She holds out her limp arms, and I bring the screaming baby over to her.

It's human. *He* is human. I clean him off as best I can with rags, and guide him into her arms. She hiccups, a weak smile pulling up the sides of her mouth. Her eyes drift up to mine.

"He made it," she whispers as the baby screams. "He's here."

CHAPTER 21

JAR'KEL

The howl of the new whelp fills my ears. I sit up in the tiny chair at the dining room table, watching for any sign of what's happening in the room.

I worry about Vavi as much as I worry about Simka. If her sister were to die, she may never be the same again, and Gorren will certainly take more drastic measures in his grief—if the bond doesn't take him first.

Finally, against my better judgment I peer into the room.

"Try to feed him," Masha is saying to Vavi, showing her how to latch the baby on. "It will help with the bleeding." But Vavi is too weak, and she falls back against the bed.

Simka holds the whelp, who continues to wail. Her father is crouched over them both, as if protecting them from the world. He cleans the newborn, rinsing off the coating of blood and creamy detritus. The whelp is much too small, even for a human. I hope it lives, or all of us will suffer Gorren's wrath.

The midwife finally stands, wiping sweat from her forehead.

"She has a chance at surviving this," she says to Simka and her father. "Let me see him." She checks the whelp over, and sighs. "It was too early. He will struggle." She starts barking orders at us. Simka fetches towels, I search for a basket, and Simka's father locates goat's milk. The midwife brings out a soft nipple made of leather and fills it with the milk, and instructs Simka how to put it in the baby's mouth.

I expected Vavi to die after losing so much blood on our long journey. Though her breaths are shallow and uneven, her chest continues rising and falling, and I have hope that I'll be wrong. The infant suckles, then stops and cries again. Simka holds it close, rocking it back and forth, and I kneel down beside her to look.

Human. It's odd, but I've seen many strange things in my time. My former captain gave birth to an orc whelp herself. This creature is soft and tiny, helpless and fragile, but as Simka cradles it, I imagine her someday holding one of our own. I put my hands on her shoulders and bracket her head between my tusks, giving her a gentle kiss on her crown.

When it seems as if Vavi is stable again, the exhausted midwife performs one last check of the baby, and leaves us with detailed instructions. She will return soon to attend to him, but he'll need special care, and she has many ingredients she'll need to fetch from Morgenzan for mother and child. But the way will be treacherous, and everyone fears the wild orcs.

"Go with her, troll," Simka's father snaps. "You will protect her and make sure she gets what she needs. It's nighttime, and there are wolves out there. Whatever is happening here..." He gestures at Simka, and then at me. "It will not go on in my house."

It's disappointing, but I expected this. Will he let Vavi return to the orc camp? What will Gorren do when his mate and offspring don't come back?

I think of the huge orc's fury and shudder. If he attacks in order to find Vavi, this village will not survive.

Before I go, Simka stops me at the front door. Her father glares but doesn't intervene as we whisper to each other.

"You must convince him to let us go back to the mountain," I tell her. "He doesn't want to risk what will happen when Gorren comes looking for his mate and whelp."

Simka shudders. "Dad won't let her go."

"I know. But he has to. I will try to convince him when I return."

Suddenly Simka has her arms wrapped around me, her face pressed into my chest. "Thank you," she whispers, drying her tears on my blood-soaked clothes. "Thank you for making sure my sister lives. Come back to me."

I smile down at her. "I will always come back for you. No matter where you go, you're stuck with me."

She lets out a tremulous laugh, and rubs the blunt end of my broken tusk once, as if for good luck, before slipping back into the house.

SIMKA

The moment Jar'kel is gone and everything is eerily quiet again, my father rounds on me. He shuts the door to the room where Vavi and the baby are sound asleep.

"I—I thought you were dead, Simka!"

"I know. I'm so sorry." I take his hand in mine, but he yanks it away. "I tried, Dad. I tried to come back. The orcs wouldn't let us go."

His eyes are bloodshot, his face red. He turns back to the closed door and I can tell he's falling apart inside. He's not angry, but devastated, and doesn't know how else to show it.

"You found her," he manages out. "After all this time." I nod. "Who's the father?"

I swallow hard. "An orc," I say quietly.

He spins around, looking like he's been slapped. "You can't be serious."

"The leader of the wild orc clan. She's... she's his mate."

Dad's fury explodes out of him. "His *what?*"

I guide him over to the table where we can sit across from each other, and I explain everything. How I found Vavi already bonded to Gorren, pregnant. How Jar'kel and I lied to survive, how I bonded with him, too. My father remains silent, eyes growing wider with every new turn in my story.

"Jar'kel was the one who insisted we bring her here. He carried her the whole way." I choke as fresh tears spring to my eyes, thinking of my troll and all he's done. "She's only alive because of him, Dad."

My father drops his head in his arms on the table, and remains there for a long time. Then he looks up at me.

"I can't believe you're married to a fucking trollkin," he says with a groan. "What is this world coming to?"

I shrug. "He's a good guy. And we're not married. Yet."

"He's as old as I am! I think." Dad rubs his eyes, and I know we're both exhausted and at the end of our ropes. Masha won't be back until tomorrow, even if they trek all night, so I get to my feet and shrug.

"So what?" I offer a smile. "He means everything to me. And if you can't see that... I can't help you."

My father's face is a mixture of hurt, rage, and then, overwhelming relief. He surges to his feet and wraps his arms around me.

"I'm so glad you're safe," he says, his shoulders shaking. "So glad."

I hug him back. "I'd never leave you, Dad."

After he's gone to bed, I return to the room where Vavi and the baby are sleeping. I feed him as much as I can, and return him to his basket. I think Vavi is unconscious until she reaches out and brushes my arm.

"Thank you," she murmurs. "Thank you, sister."

I kiss her forehead. "You know I'd do anything for you."

I just hope that Jar'kel will return to me, too.

JAR'KEL

The midwife and I walk in silence. There's nothing for us to talk about, and I appreciate that she doesn't try to make petty conversation. She rides Simka's little mule, Fio, who reluctantly carries her. He's only doing it for Simka, same as I am.

Showing my face in Morgenzan again is a risk, a big one, but it's one I'm willing to take to ensure Vavi and her whelp's safety. If something happened to them, it would break Simka—and things will go much more poorly for everyone if she doesn't survive.

Dawn comes, and the sun's nearly filled the sky before the walled city comes into view. These mountains carry new meaning for me now, knowing what power lies underneath them, what danger the trollkin are putting themselves and everyone else in by digging deeper and deeper into the earth. If the Grand Chieftain got his hands on even one pot's full of that glowing magic... we'd all be well and truly fucked.

I untie my cloak, the cloak Simka gave me that fateful night in Fio's pen, and approach the gates to the city bearing my corporal's badge and coat. The guards salute me.

"Corporal," they say automatically.

One of them squints. "Hey, wait. You're that one troll who disappeared."

I nod, then gesture at the midwife. "We need the city alchemist right away. Whatever she requires. There's an emergency in one of the villages."

The guard points the midwife in the right direction, and I'm about to follow her when the two of the stop me.

"I think the commander's going to want to see you," the second guard says, dropping his halberd down in front of me. "You were gone a long time, *corporal*."

I massage my temples. Fuck.

The commander of the Morgenzan city guard is a stout human with a black beard as thick as Fio's coat.

"Commander Kallon," I greet him when I'm not-so-gently pushed into his office in the city council hall. I was "escorted" here, and I insisted on bringing Fio with me and tying him up outside. Simka would be furious if I lost her beloved ass.

The commander tilts his head when he sees me. "Oh, the missing corporal. You made it back alive."

"Yes, sir." That's all I offer. He arches an eyebrow at me, tapping his quill on the desk.

"Where have you been? You went to one of those human villages after the fire and vanished into the night."

I shrug. "Let's just say I was kidnapped." There's no version of this interaction where I get out of Morgenzan safely. It's sickening, really, to know I've just found Simka, and I won't be able to return to her. "There was no way for me to get back, not until the orcs released me."

Commander Kallon's eyebrows shoot up. "You know the location of the wild orc camp?" A wide smile spreads across his face as he surges to his feet. "This is fantastic news, corporal. This could finally turn the tide against them. There've been at least two more raids since you left, each one more devastating than the last."

I just sigh. I know what comes next, and I feel my age now more than ever.

"Show us," the commander says, unrolling a map on his desk. It's the Blue Crags, or what we know of them given how treacherous it is to explore them. He hands me his quill.

But I drop it onto the map, letting it drip ink across the peaks. I may not have any loyalty to Gorren or his clan, but I am loyal to Simka and Vavi. Gorren would surely be murdered if I revealed where they've hidden their camp, and I can't do that to Vavi.

"You have to make the Grand Chieftain stop the mining operation," I say instead. The commander furrows his brow like the words are foreign to him. "That's why the orcs are attacking. They're protecting this mountain. They won't stop until everyone working that mine is dead."

Every last shred of sympathy or camaraderie the commander might have felt for me vanishes in an instant. He walks around his desk, hands clasped behind his back, a deadly look in his eyes.

"I harbor no love for trollkin," he says, coming to a stop in front of me. He's trying to intimidate me by getting so close, but it's hard to take him seriously when I have to tilt my head down to look him in the face. "And I don't enjoy sending my soldiers to protect a mine that isn't even ours, risking their lives to defend someone else's riches. But it's part of the job, corporal. It's the oath that both of us swore. We keep the peace. We protect the city and everything that happens around it."

"What about those human villages?" I ask, keeping my voice cool and calm. "Young people were stolen, food stores raided, and you did nothing."

He bristles, the hair practically rising up off his head. "The Grand Chieftain is providing for our funding, our resources, and our soldiers. This is how we keep our *jobs*. Defending little hamlets from barbarians doesn't pay the city guard's bills."

So that's it. Those are the principles I once prided myself on serving. I understand even more now why my former captain handed me her badge and stepped aside from her responsibilities. This is a job that takes and takes, reinforcing power, all while Gorren and his clan defend this mountain and its ancient mystery from those who would take advantage of it.

When I say nothing in response, the commander gives a disappointed shake of his head. "You know what comes next, don't you, corporal? Now that you've deserted your post and you refuse to disclose the location of the camp?"

I nod, sealing my fate. This is exactly what I had feared when I finally embraced my bond with Simka, when I let her inside me— that something like this would happen and I'd leave her all alone.

But I wouldn't take back a moment of my time with her.

CHAPTER 22

SIMKA

I am pure anxiety as I sit at Vavi's side, holding the baby in my arms. My sister's been in and out of consciousness all night, never awake long enough to even give him a name. When his eyes are open—which is rare, between the sleeping and the crying —they look just like hers. He's almost a copy of her, with our dark hair and light brown skin, but he doesn't have the fat cheeks and pudgy body I've always seen babies have. He's much too light, and far smaller than he should be. I feed him as often as possible, prepared with the nipple and milk when he wakes up again calling for his mother.

Dad and I take turns trying to sleep, as difficult as it is when the baby is sobbing his heart out and then falling eerily quiet, as if it takes too much energy for him to cry. Vavi's bleeding has stopped, but still her breaths are shallow and labored.

The morning of the following day, the midwife reappears at the door. But she's all alone.

"Where's Jar'kel?" I ask, trying to keep my panic at bay in case there's a reasonable explanation. He should be here with her. He was her escort.

Masha shakes her head. "The troll was taken away by the guards at the gates." She seems unbothered by this as she steps inside with her basket of ingredients and attends to her patient.

I stand in the doorway, staring out into the snow, my heart racing and my limbs heavy with dread. Once they learn where he's been, surely they'll interrogate him for information. Will he reveal the location of the camp? Will he put my sister's mate in danger to save himself?

No. I know his soul now, and what lies underneath his stiff, heavy armor. He wouldn't do that to me or to her. Which means... he's a deserter. He'll be their captive until he gives them what they want, and they'll use whatever means necessary to try to get it from him.

I imagine my Jar'kel strung up by his hands while they poke and prod him, testing how much pain he can take, pulling out his tusk by the root, and my body tenses up to fight. I will kill them if they touch a hair on him. I can't let this happen.

"Simka?" Vavi asks in a breathy voice as I sprint for the bedroom door. "Where are you going?"

I pause briefly to take her hand and kiss her forehead. "I have to go," I say. "To the camp. I need Gorren."

She blinks at me. "What for? I'll be all right soon." Masha brings the baby over and settles him in her arms. Her face lights up in a way I've never seen before, and she gazes down at him with pure, pristine love. "So will Varn."

I pause. "Varn?" I lean down briefly to take his tiny hand in mine, and squeeze his little fingers. "Good choice, sis."

She smiles up at me as the baby starts to cry again. "Just wait for me to get some strength back, and we can go together."

I shake my head rapidly. "I'm going now. I have to ask Gorren to help me get Jar'kel back."

Vavi's light dims. "He's gone?"

I nod. "Taken into custody by the city guard. I don't know what they'll do to him to get what they want... but I'm not going to wait to find out."

"After all Jar'kel has done for me, I know Gorren will help," Vavi says, offering me a reassuring smile. "Be careful. I want you to come back to us. Jar'kel, too. He's my family now as much as you are."

"Thank you." I turn around to find Dad standing in the doorway, his eyes just as red around the edges as mine from so little sleep.

"You're going after that troll?" he asks, the disappointment obvious on his face.

"I'm sorry, Dad." I hug him, and he hugs me back so tight I worry I might break in his arms. "I have to."

He releases me and searches my eyes, as if trying to find out if I truly mean the words. Then, he grunts in understanding. Dad goes into his own room, and I hear shuffling. When he returns, he's got a short sword in his hand inside a leather sheath. He wraps the belt around my waist, tightening it, and then gives me one more pat.

"Go get him," he says. "And you'd better come back, grouchy old troll or not."

I offer him what I can of a smile. "Of course."

It will take much longer to reach the camp without Fio, but I know my legs are strong and will carry me there. I have no choice.

JAR'KEL

The inside of my jail cell reeks. I expected it to be hard and cold, as I'd seen the prison for myself when I first arrived in Morgenzan.

What I hadn't expected was how filthy and disgusting it would be, too.

I'm most offended, though, that they took my mittens.

The city guard has managed to take one of the wild orcs captive. From the little he's been able to tell me, the commander has tortured him over and over again for information. But he won't give in, no matter how many fingers they break or long needles they drive through his flesh. He'll be loyal to Gorren until the end, even while he's clinging to life in the cell next to mine.

Some of the smell is coming from him, but the rest... it seems to be seeping in through the walls. I cover my nose as I settle back against the rough stone of the cell. There are two blankets in one corner and a receptacle for waste, but that's it.

"It's the rats," the orc in the next cell tells me as I plug my nose again. "They come in here after crumbs of food, crawl into the walls and can't get out. Then they die."

Lovely.

"What did you do?" he asks, peering at my corporal's jacket. "You're one of them."

I shrug. "It's a long story."

The orc laughs, then interrupts himself with a gagging cough. "We got time, troll."

Not like I have anything else to do, and there's only one guard at the jail sitting far out of earshot, so I start at the beginning.

The orc, whose name I've gathered is Rugar, listens in complete silence as I finish my tale. I spared him some of the worse details, including the way my mate claimed me. All that is for me and me alone.

"If you hadn't told me so much about the camp, I'd think you were lying," he says, shaking his head. "But after all that, now you're stuck here for the rest of your miserable life."

I have to chuckle at that. "Yup. Fucked, isn't it?"

He snorts. "I doubt that woman of yours will take this lying down, though, if what you've told me about her is true."

This thought hadn't crossed my mind, and dread seeps into my veins. If Simka does come for me... that would be the worst possible outcome. She'd end up rotting in a cell next to me, tortured until she gives up the camp's location.

Rugar must see the dark look that comes over my face, because he says, "Hey, old man. She doesn't sound like some idiot whelp. She won't come without a plan."

I can only hope he's right. My mate may be a little rash, but she's also smart and wily. I have no choice but to believe in her.

SIMKA

When I finally make it back to the wild orc camp, I'm sweating from every last pore. The guards rush out, weapons at the ready, and I wave them off in irritation.

"I need to see Gorren," I growl. "Right now."

They exchange looks, then sheath their swords and nod for me to follow.

"Be careful," one of them tells me in broken Freysian. "He's angry."

I'm not surprised to hear this, so I nod as we make our way through the rows of tents. When I reach the one he shared with Vavi, raised voices filter out the tent flap. I peel it open and find Gorren bearing down on one of the other orcs, letting off a string of what I can only imagine are curses in Trollkin. He freezes when he sees me.

"Vavi?" he rushes over to me. "Is Vavi all right?"

I nod. "She's going to live. So will the baby." I offer him a tentative smile. "His name is Varn."

Immense relief cascades across Gorren's face, and that stern mouth of his is swept up into a huge smile. Suddenly he pulls me into a hug, squeezing me tight. "Thank you," he says, voice choked. "Thank you, sister of Vavi." Then he pulls away, confused. "Where is corporal?"

I wince at the question. I hope he doesn't turn me away. "That's why I'm here. I need your help. The city guard took him prisoner."

Gorren's eyes fly wide, and then his mouth twists down in a deep scowl. "He knows."

I shake my head fervently. "He won't tell. I know it." Jar'kel would never crack. "But we have to go get him now, before they try to cut it out of him."

Gorren steps back from me, and slowly shakes his head. "I am sorry."

"...Sorry?" I ask, my heart sinking. I've wasted all this time coming here. "Why?"

"Cannot help you." He turns away towards the map in the middle of the room. "Too dangerous."

"But he saved Vavi and the baby!" My voice is high and pinched. I grab his sleeve, forcing him to look at me. "The only reason they're alive is thanks to him! It's the least you could do."

Gorren's shoulders clench tight. He can't really be refusing to help me after everything we've done—after everything *Jar'kel* has done.

"Attack Morgenzan? Impossible." Gorren turns to me, brow knitted. "Many would die. Cannot do it."

I want to simply sit on the floor and cry. As much as I hate it... he's right. The walls of Morgenzan are impenetrable, and as numerous as the wild orcs are, they wouldn't stand a chance against the entire city guard.

I sag onto one of the chairs and cover my face, imagining my Jar'kel trapped in a prison cell while they try to pry the camp's location from his gritted teeth. My stomach turns over.

"We have to save him." I can tell I'm on the edge of breaking. "Please. I need him."

Gorren looks at me with pity, because he understands. "I know. I need Vavi also." With a sad shake of his head, he returns to the map.

I bury my face in my hands, trying to keep my emotions under control long enough to think. What would Jar'kel do? He's more experienced in these kinds of things. If I could just think like he does... maybe I'd have a chance at this.

Wait. I remember our plan to escape the orc camp once upon a time. *Distractions are the best way to overcome a disadvantage*, he'd said. If you have a bigger or more numerous opponent, trying to beat them head-to-head will never work. Diverting their attention and sneaking right past them is the only way to win.

"Wait." I jump to my feet. "Gorren. What if you attacked the mine? Bring the entire force. You want to destroy it anyway, right? I think my goals and yours could align."

He just shrugs. "We tried. We lost. City guard is large and we are small."

I try to think of what else I could offer to make my proposal appealing, what would make it possible. What other resources does Gorren have at his disposal?

Then I remember the hot spring. The magic carved into the walls.

My eyes rise up to his. "The magic. It's down there, right? Underneath the mine?" He nods uneasily. "What if... what if we used it?"

His eyes narrow dangerously. "It is sacred," he says. "Precious. Dangerous."

"I know. But it's also powerful. Maybe that's what's been missing all along. You aren't strong enough to take the mine alone, but what if you used the magic you have?" I know about the pot he keeps under the table, too. "Maybe you shouldn't be afraid of it. Rather than trying to pick apart the trollkin one piece at a time, what if you got rid of them for good?"

He snorts derisively. "Too dangerous! Magic is hidden on purpose."

"And you are protecting it," I remind him. "Surely your ancestors would approve of doing whatever you have to do to keep it safe from the Grand Chieftain?"

At first it looks like Gorren will outright refuse me, but he pauses for a moment to think it through.

"Please," I whisper. "Please. I need to free him. Jar'kel is... he's my everything. I know you understand."

The big orc's eyes search mine for a long time. Then, after the silence becomes deafening, he nods.

"Wild Simka," he mutters. "Same as Vavi. Fine. We will do this." He narrows his eyes at me. "Get your mate."

I grin widely. "Thank you."

He shrugs. "For my son. I give him a world safe for him."

That's all right with me.

CHAPTER 23

JAR'KEL

I don't know how much time has passed in this dark place. The prison is lit only by a flickering torch, and the guard attends to us briefly to deposit meals at random intervals. Having seen the wounds on the orc in the next cell, I know what awaits me. They're much more barbaric here in the frigid mountains than we are in the desert. My former captain would never have tortured to get what she wants.

I'm not surprised when two guards come for me with metal shackles. They push open the cell door and grab me roughly, wrenching my arms behind my back. There's no point fighting and hurting myself more than necessary, so I walk along obediently as they lead me down the row of cells. Rugar gives me a grim nod of encouragement.

We go up two flights of stairs before emerging into the light, which I don't get to enjoy for long before they lead me to a new room: one equipped with a steel table and leather straps.

Commander Kallon stands with his arms crossed, awaiting me.

Beside him is a tall trolless wearing a pair of goggles and a coat stained brown with blood.

I can only hope that my mate can't feel my pain.

I'm flung down on the table, my jacket and shirt torn off. Then I'm strapped in with my hands still shackled over my head. The trolless steps forward with what looks like an extremely long sewing needle in her hand. Her expression is disturbingly blank as Commander Kallon appears over her shoulder.

"I'll give you another chance, corporal," he says. "Tell us where to find them."

I shrug and say nothing. The commander gestures to his attendant.

"Let's see if we can get this old boy squeaking," he says. She nods curtly, and positions the needle over my sternum. The point reminds me of Simka's dagger, how she pressed it into my chest, her eyes wild with inner fire. I try to think of her as it digs in.

That's when we hear an immense *boom!* Underneath our feet, the very ground shakes.

"What?" Commander Kallon narrows his eyes. "Earthquake?"

Suddenly, the door bangs open. "Commander!" someone says, breathless.

"What is it?" he snarls, spinning around. "I'm in the middle of something."

I tilt my head up as one of the city guards stands panting in the doorway. "They're here! The wild orcs have come. All of them. And they're attacking the mine with..." The guard shakes her head, like she doesn't understand what's happening for herself. "With dynamite. And fire. It's chaos, sir."

The commander stiffens. "They've never used dynamite before." He growls low in his throat. "Fuck. All right, round everyone up. We're mounting a defense, *now*." Annoyed, he gestures at me. "Throw this traitor back in his cell. I'll deal with him later."

I blink in surprise as the woman with the needle retreats from her work. She's just as perplexed as I am. Without another word, the commander runs from the room, leaving us alone.

I can't help my grin. My Simka, as fierce as she is clever. Whatever she has planned, she will win.

SIMKA

Gorren has decided it's do-or-die. I only hope that he survives, because my sister might never forgive me.

"You are right, Simka," he says as we stand high above Morgenzan, the whole clan standing behind him. "Why have magic if not for protecting ourselves, and the secret of the mountains?"

He is one of the few orcs who can handle it safely, having a human mate of his own. The others stand at the front, many having brought their partners along with them to fight. This is a final stand. Gorren has even imparted me a tiny amount for myself to help in my plan to break out Jar'kel. I'll need a way inside the city, and then the prison.

I nod. "I think that's exactly why it exists." No, I'm certain of it now. That's what the hot spring cave was telling us with those strange carvings. It's why Vavi was drawn to Gorren. What we're doing isn't wrong—it's the opposite. We were given the gift of magic so we could use it to protect ourselves, each other, and this incredible power.

Gorren nods in agreement. He draws his massive battle axe, and gestures for me to go on ahead. "Go rescue your troll," he says, the clay pot clutched tight under his arm. "We'll keep the city guard plenty busy."

"Thank you." With a final salute, I take off down the mountainside, clutching the bottle in my pocket tight.

No one spares me a second glance when I make it to the front gate of the city. Morgenzan looms high overhead, crawling up the immense mountainside that's pockmarked with doorways. I'd assumed the prison would be below city council, but now I'm not so sure.

And if it is, how would I possibly get down there? I reach into my pocket and palm the tiny bottle. I just hope this stuff will work.

The guards are stepping out to greet me and ask my business when an immense *boom!* echoes through the valley. Everyone cranes their necks to look into the sky as a great billow of smoke bursts into the air, high above the mine.

Perfect. Just what I needed. Gorren has begun.

"What the hell?" One of the guards drops his hand to the hilt of his sword. "Wild orc attack?"

"Has to be," the other one answers. They've forgotten all about me by the time I scurry in through the gate right past them.

Great. Now where? Another massive explosion rocks the earth underneath us, and surprised screams rise up from people going about their business. Even though the mine is in the next mountain over, whatever Gorren is doing, it's enough to rattle my very bones.

I race past townspeople, who are all staring up in horror as more smoke fills the air. The city guards assemble, barking orders at one another, racing towards the city gates. The ground shakes as soldiers lead horses from the nearby stables to join the force that will confront Gorren and his clan.

Now, picking my way up the path that bends and curves around the mountain, there's no one in my way. If only I knew where to find Jar'kel.

Right. I have magic, too. I duck to the side of a bridge that crosses a waterfall, so I'm hidden from passers-by. Taking the bottle from my pocket, I dribble some of the glowing purple liquid into my hand, just a droplet.

Say what you want, Gorren had instructed. *And it will happen.*

I close my eyes, squeezing the droplet in my hand. *Show me where to find Jar'kel,* I think. *Show me where they're keeping him.*

I open my hand again, and a tiny ball of glowing light rises out of my palm. It hovers for a moment, and then, like a bolt of lightning, it races away.

"Shit!" I jump onto the bridge, frightening an old lady with a basket, and sprint past her after the little speck of light. It zooms up the path, and I follow close behind, pumping my legs as hard as I can to keep pace. Rather than heading up the mountain toward city council, the bouncing ball of light dives off onto a side road, one I would've never thought to take. Already my breath is coming ragged as I run at full-tilt, careening around a curve and dodging a wagon laden with goods. Someone shouts at me, but I keep going after the glowing purple dot.

It stops abruptly at a low entryway, sealed shut by a heavy wood and iron door. Then, it winks out of existence.

"Great." I try the knob but, as I expected, it's locked. There's no way I'm getting inside this thing without a key. Underneath me, the ground rumbles again, and more smoke fills the sky. "All right, glowy shit." I dribble a little more out of the bottle into my hand. I close my eyes and think, *Open this door.*

Once more the purple goo rises out of my palm, and then the shape of it... shifts. It warps and stretches until it's roughly the size and shape of a key, and then it slides into the lock. With a groan, the knob turns, and the door opens in front of me.

The key dissipates into smoke. Damn, this stuff is useful.

I yank open the heavy door. On the other side the hallway is dark, and I fumble my way inside to close it behind me. A single torch sits in a sconce on the wall, lighting up a set of steep steps that descend into the darkness.

He's down there. I know it. I can feel his presence in my bones.

Snatching the torch off the wall, I take the stairs, keeping my eyes peeled for anyone around. But Gorren's distraction has worked, and there are no guards in sight when I reach the bottom.

Ahead of me is a long hallway, running alongside a set of iron jail cells. I creep down the row, peering inside each one, but they're all empty—until I reach the end.

In the second-to-last cell I catch sight of an orc slumped over against a wall. He's covered in dried blood, and I'm not sure if he's breathing. By his sparse clothing, he must be one of Gorren's clan. Then his chest heaves, once, and I breathe out with relief.

"Simka?"

The familiar sound of Jar'kel's voice makes my head jerk. He's standing up inside his cell, the very last one, his red eyes round and his mouth parted in surprise.

"Jar'kel!" I move to the next iron door. Behind it, Jar'kel is shirtless, a dribble of fresh blood running down his chest. Besides that, though, he doesn't look any worse for the wear. I rush to the bars and put my hands through them, reaching for him. He shakes his head like he doesn't believe it's me, and takes my five fingers in his four, weaving them together.

"What are you doing here?" he hisses, glancing down the hallway. "They're going to catch you."

As if on cue, the whole mountain around us shakes. His eyes get even bigger, and I grin.

"Gorren's providing me a nice little distraction." I pause. "Not so little, maybe."

"How did you get Gorren involved in this?" Jar'kel asks. "It's a big risk for him." My troll is a little dirty, but otherwise he looks like himself. I'm glad they haven't had a chance to hurt him yet. I don't know what I would do. Probably kill them.

"He wants to end this for good," I say. "We have a plan, though."

Jar'kel arches his eyebrow, and a smirk pulls at his lip. The orc in the next cell slowly drags himself up to his feet.

"Gorren?" he asks, then speaks a string of Trollkin I can't understand.

"He's asking what the wild orcs are doing," Jar'kel translates for me.

"Gorren's using the magic to take the mine." I squeeze his hand once more before letting it go. "Now I have to get you out of here. Give me a moment to concentrate."

He gives me a look like he doesn't recognize me. "You don't have a key, Simka."

"Don't need one." I fumble around with the bottle, and when he sees the glowing magic inside, he backs away. Unstoppering it, I pour a tiny bit more into my hand. After this, I really only have one wish left, if that's what I could call it. *Unlock this cell door*, I think hard. *Let him out.*

"You brought some of that with you?" Jar'kel says, voice nervous. "Simka, that stuff is danger—"

The glowing purple blob zips out of my hand, hurling itself into the keyhole. For a moment, nothing happens. And then the metal turns red hot—and starts to melt away. I take a few steps back, too, unnerved by the molten metal dripping down onto the floor.

The cell door opens with a rusty creak, nothing left of the lock but melted iron. Jar'kel and I exchange a look. He steps toward the opening as if he doesn't believe it's real, and slides out to avoid the hot metal.

I can't help it. I jump on him with my whole body, wrapping my arms around his neck, dragging him in close to taste his mouth again. He returns my kiss just as eagerly, lifting me up by my rear so my hips are pressed tightly against his. I'm met with a groan when I wrap my legs around him, clinging to him as he drinks me up.

"Simka," he finally says breathlessly, lowering me back to the ground. "We have to get out of here." Then he glances at the orc in the other cell, who's been watching us with weary eyes. "And him, too."

I glance down at the bottle in my hand, only one little droplet left. If we run into any obstacles on our way out of the city... I won't be able to help.

"He was tortured for the location of the camp, but he didn't give in." Jar'kel gives the other orc an appreciative nod.

"Fine," I say with a sigh, and dribble the last bit of magic into my hand. "This is all we've got, though." Then I make the same wish: *Open this door.*

Another melted lock later, the second cell door swings open. Jar'kel runs inside to help the orc up to his feet, but he's weak, injured, and malnourished. I pull his other arm over my shoulders, and together, we hobble out of the prison, hoping Gorren's done a good enough job of drawing the city guard away that we can make it out alive.

Chapter 24

Jar'kel

My wild Simka. My fireball, my sharpened spear. She grunts as she helps Rugar up the steps of the prison, still holding the torch in her other hand. She came for me ready to fight, a short sword at her side and a bottle of dynamite in her hand.

I've never admired someone so much.

When we reach the top, I shove the prison door open and we emerge into the sunlight. Oh, sunlight. I wasn't down there very long, but it was long enough to make me grateful for the sun's rays on my skin.

I also realize just how frigid it is without the marvelous cloak Simka gave me. I wonder where it is now.

Maybe she'll give me another one.

Morgenzan spreads out below, while above us, smoke fills the sky. Another quake shakes the ground and Rugar stumbles, but I manage to keep him upright.

Luckily, Gorren's distraction is working, and the townspeople are too busy whispering amongst themselves and watching the distant mountainside to pay too much attention to us. When they do see us, their eyes grow wide, but they step aside to let us through. We must look like hell, I think. At least there are no guards around to question us.

We make our way steadily down the road toward the base of the mountain. Up ahead are the city gates. When we reach the bottom, my eyes are drawn to the stable.

"Fio," I hiss to myself. Shit. We can't leave Simka's ass here, or she'll never forgive me. I ease Rugar down to a sitting position, and Simka tilts her head. "Fio must be in there," I explain.

She gives me a wide smile and charges off into the stable. While she's gone, Rugar and I stare upward, aghast, as a ball of fire shoots into the sky and more people scream. Nearby, there's an orc carrying a big pack on his back, his head tilted back while he watches the show.

"Damn it," he says, pushing up the big goggles he was wearing. "Just got off the train to go and see that place, and now it's up in flames?"

I tilt my head at him. "You came for the mine? Are you a new worker?"

"No. I was looking for something in that there mountain, but I don't think I'll be finding it now." He snaps his fingers.

With a snicker I say, "I don't think so, either."

Only a few moments later Simka emerges with her mule in tow. When she reaches us, Simka nods at Rugar. "Fio can carry him. It'll be easier to travel that way."

I nod in agreement, and between the two of us, we're able to heft the injured orc up onto Fio's back. The fuzzy coot isn't pleased about it, but Simka's here now, and he'll do whatever she asks. Even as another explosion rattles the ground, he looks utterly unfazed by it.

With Rugar taken care of, we make our way to the high walls of the city. For a moment, it looks like there's no one at the guard posts, and I think maybe Gorren's gambit has worked. We'll be able to pass freely through, and return to Simka's village. We'll get out of this alive.

"Halt!" Someone steps out in front of us—one of the human guards who must have stayed behind, the single one of my colleagues left to defend the city while the rest are off fighting orcs. Damn it.

I didn't want it to come to this. He's simply a cog in a much greater machine, just like I was. He doesn't know any better. This is his job, and he likely has a family here in the city.

But I'm done playing the Grand Chieftain's games. When the guard approaches us, I offer him one chance.

"We're leaving," I tell him cooly. He looks us up and down.

"You're that prisoner." He reaches for the hilt of his blade. "There's no way I'm letting you—"

Before he can draw it, Simka has her sword out and pointed at his throat. Somehow, she snuck up on him while he was focused on me. He freezes.

"Now," she says in a low, scathing voice. "You'll let us go, *now*." She gestures up at the mountain. Rocks are tumbling down from the highest peaks as it shakes. "I think you have much bigger problems."

The man swallows hard, looking at me, then at Rugar and Simka. Uneasily, he backs away, and gestures for us to go through. She lowers her sword, returns it to its sheath, and takes Fio by the lead rope.

I found the best woman there is.

As a trophy, I take the guard's sword with me.

Simka

It's a long way to the village back the way I came. We walk all night, but as hard as I try to keep my eyes open and continue plodding along through the snow, the fatigue catches up to me.

"Simka." I didn't realize I'd stopped moving until Jar'kel says my name. He catches my arm as I tip over. Rugar is asleep on Fio, who doesn't seem all too pleased to be used as a bed. "Here. Let me carry you."

I gasp with indignance. "I can walk!"

"You're falling asleep on your feet." He turns his back toward me and gestures that I should climb on. I hesitate, because what if he thinks I'm weak for needing his help?

But if I can be weak with anyone, it's Jar'kel.

I wrap my arms around his neck and he hefts me up, pulling my legs around his hips. Once I'm settled, he continues walking, and within a few steps I'm drifting off into sleep.

I wake up to the sound of someone calling my name.

"Simka!" I jerk upright, and Jar'kel almost drops me. He crouches down to let me slide off, and when I manage to get my feet under me, I find Dad running towards me.

"You're back." He glances up at Jar'kel, who towers over him. Dad offers him a faint smile. "Thank you."

Jar'kel just nods.

"Who's this?" Dad asks warily, eyeballing the damaged orc we brought along with us.

"Someone who needs help." Jar'kel pulls Rugar off Fio's back and helps him stand up.

"Another trollkin?" Dad sighs, shaking his head. "Are we going to take them all in like lost dogs?"

The three of us follow him back to the house, where we deposit poor Fio in the pen. I make sure to give him extra hay and grain, and he happily munches as we head inside the house.

Once we have a pile of blankets made up for Rugar on the floor by the hearth, I go to the healer to get him some help. The grizzled man is reluctant to work on an orc, and we make sure not to tell him he's part of the wild orc clan. Jar'kel makes up a story about him being a member of the city guard injured in the attack, and reluctantly, the healer sets to cleaning Rugar's wounds and fighting the infection that's been spreading.

"He's got a good chance, but I won't guarantee anything," he says.

That's the best we can do.

Vavi is still bedridden, but after the midwife brought back supplies, she can sit up and nurse little Varn. He's still small and fragile, but he'll grow bigger, Masha promises. As long as he eats, he'll be the average baby soon enough.

"What was all the ruckus?" Dad finally asks us, when everyone is settled in.

"The wild orcs attacked the mine. All of them. They plan to destroy it this time." I have to hope they succeeded.

Dad stares at me. "That's a death sentence. They won't stand a chance."

"I think they do." I have to hope Gorren accomplished what he set out to do, and our crazy gambit was successful.

"Gorren will succeed, if he has magic at his disposal." Jar'kel speaks with an undeniable certainty. His gaze drifts to the bedroom, where Vavi and the baby are asleep. "And he has much to protect."

Dad's eyes dart to mine. I still don't think he believes me about what we saw up there, but he will once word travels from Morgenzan.

I can see the deep lines and dark shadows under Jar'kel's eyes, so I get up and rub his shoulders. "You should get some sleep," I tell him. He looks like he's about to object, but I silence him with a kiss. Dad makes a disgusted noise. "Come on. You look like death."

Jar'kel chuckles darkly. "I have already avoided the grave once today."

My troll follows me into the bedroom, where he barely fits in my tiny bed as his big, four-toed feet hang off the end. He's asleep almost the moment his head hits the pillow.

"I'm going to have to get used to him, won't I?" Dad asks when I return to the main room, where Rugar sleeps restlessly in the corner.

"Yep." I pat the top of his hand. "Jar'kel makes me happy, Dad. And I'd do anything for him."

"I can tell," he says with a roll of his eyes. "Get your own place, though. I'm already tired of watching you."

Jar'kel

I awake to the sound of shouting outside the house.

When I rush from the room, Simka and her father are already ahead of me. Out in the street, it's impossible to mistake Gorren's powerful bellow.

"Where is Vavi?" he demands. Some villagers run back to their homes to hide, but others stand in the way, their guns aimed and ready to fire at the amassed force of wild orcs.

"Shit," I mutter. This doesn't look good for anyone.

"Wait!" Simka calls out. She sprints towards Gorren, holding her hands out in front of the villagers. "Wait, hold your fire!"

When the huge orc sees her, his rage seems to cool. The whole clan stands behind him, weapons drawn, waiting for the humans to start the fight.

"Vavi's here," Simka says, settling a hand on his arm. He visibly softens under her touch. I wonder briefly if, as Vavi's closest family, they share some sort of bond of their own. "She's at my house. Come on."

Those villagers who were prepared to defend their home raise their weapons again as Gorren comes closer.

"They're not here for a fight," I say. A few of them jerk to look at me.

"You're that troll. The one who helped save Vavi." One of the men with a gun lowers it.

I nod. "He's just here for the woman. Then they'll go." I glance up at Gorren. "Right? Once you have her, you'll leave this village alone?"

The big orc grunts in agreement. "We will leave," he says.

Simka runs back to her house, and when she returns, she's leading a hobbling Vavi. Gorren's face breaks into a huge, relieved smile. He picks up his mate in one swoop, and she giggles as he brings her and the baby in close. He kisses her face all over, and then setting her down, examines the tiny creature in her arms. His mouth falls open.

"Human?"

She laughs, and it's a bright, vibrant sound. "Strange, isn't it?"

Gorren leans down to breathe in the baby's smell, and his whole body relaxes, as if a great weight has fallen off his shoulders. "Perfect."

As the family reunites, Simka and I bring out Rugar and lead him to the others, so they can take him with them back to the camp. Then Gorren turns to us.

"Thank you." His grin grows even wider. "We drove the trollkin out. The mine has collapsed, and everyone in it has fled, or... won't be a problem anymore."

I cringe, thinking of all those who probably died in the rockfall. Surely there were many casualties among the trollkin and the city guard alike. I hope many of them realized how outnumbered they were early and retreated.

But that's one head cut off the Grand Chieftain's great hydra, and the mystery at the bottom of the mountain is safe once again.

Gorren slaps Simka on the shoulder. "A wild idea from a wild woman. Was a big victory." Then his eyes land on me. "And you, troll. You saved my woman, and returned one of my clansmen." He thumps his chest with his fist.

"Simka would never have forgiven me if I didn't," I tell him.

"Never ." Gorren turns around and roars to his clan. "To the mountains!" he calls out.

"To the mountains!" they echo back.

Simka and Vavi exchange a hug. "I'll visit really soon," Simka says, giving Varn a kiss on the forehead. "I promise."

Their father is much less eager to see Vavi go, but he hugs her and demands that she visit as soon as possible.

And then the orcs are gone, leaving the village in peace again. My human takes my hand, and her fingers are perfectly warm wrapped around my thumb.

"Jar'kel?" she asks.

I glance down at her. "Yes?"

"Will you stay here? With me?"

I didn't think she'd ask this question, because I assumed she already knew the answer. So I stoop down and bring her small, round face between my hands.

"I will always be where you are," I tell her, running a finger down her soft cheek. "Always. You can't get rid of me now. But I might need you to make me a new pair of mittens."

Her laugh is like the Blue Crags themselves, wild and free.

CHAPTER 25

SIMKA

With Vavi gone, we finally have my room to ourselves. My father is forced to admit that I'm a grown woman —with grown woman needs—and tells us goodnight with an irritated grumble.

When we're finally alone, I push the two small beds together into one slightly bigger one, and Jar'kel gets a mischievous grin.

"I haven't said thank you yet," he murmurs, plopping me down in a sitting position on the edge. "For saving my ass from that prison cell."

"You don't need to," I say. I'd walk through fire for him. "But I won't refuse a token of your appreciation."

Jar'kel chuckles as he kneels down in front of me, hooking his thumbs in the hem of my pants. He pulls them down, sliding them off each leg, kissing my skin as he reveals it. He nudges me between the knees with his good tusk, urging them apart. I scoot forward so he can get even better access to me, and he licks his lips.

"Good," he says, nipping the inside of my thigh. "Tell me what you want."

"I want your mouth," I say in a bossy tone. His grin spreads as he reaches between my legs, just brushing his fingers over my sex. He trails them down my lower lips, then plies them apart to rub my sensitive button. He goes easy and slow, the way he always does, getting me ready for him. My troll is no impatient "whelp," as he would say. No, he has all the time in the world to pleasure me.

But I want him, and I want him now. I tangle my hands in his short, blue hair, pulling him towards me. He laughs outright before burying his face in my pussy, sucking at my clit, ducking his tongue inside me. It's not enough, though. I want more, and more, and more. I want him always, inside me, around me, showing me all of that soft heart lying underneath his hard surface.

"Please," I finally whimper when he slides in one finger, and then two, stroking the place he knows drives me wild. I try to keep in my cries as he flicks his tongue back and forth, tormenting me.

"Please what?" he says. "Use your words, Simka."

"Please put it inside me." I'm too impatient now after everything that's happened. I want to be joined with him again, right where I belong.

"Hmm." Jar'kel sits back on his heels, his hand still sliding in and out of me. "I suppose you did ask nicely. And what kind of mate would I be if I refused you?" Withdrawing his fingers, he sticks them both in his mouth and sucks them thoroughly clean. Then he pushes me down onto the bed and pins me with his body.

Once my shirt's off, he's attending to each of my breasts, rolling them in his hands and nibbling my nipples. I buck my hips, annoyed at how long he's taking, and he laughs at me in that low rumble.

Leaving me splayed in front of him, he removes his own clothes, until my scarred troll with all his sinewy muscle is bared.

He takes his cock in hand, stroking it as he gazes down at me, and I gasp just at the sight of him. I wonder if I'll ever get used to how beautiful he is, how perfectly he was made for me and I was made for him.

He kneels on the bed and places himself between my thighs. I marvel again at the size of that immense, blue cock.

"How does that fit?" I ask, reaching down to take it in my palm and squeeze. He groans under my hand.

"Very well," he says, his smug smirk pulling up his good tusk. He's already leaking for me, and I smear it around his wide head before guiding it down to that hot, dripping place where he belongs.

It's a tight fit, like it always is. I moan and twist as he pulls me open, demanding I stretch for him. My body complies, allowing him to shove himself deep on his first thrust. I can't hold in my cry, because he feels perfect, so perfect, and I yank his head down by his tusk to kiss him.

"You're mine," I tell him.

He groans, pulling almost all the way out just to bury himself deep once again.

"I know," he says, finding his place inside me. "Just as you are mine."

JAR'KEL

How it feels to be connected to my woman again—there is no greater pleasure or joy in the world.

She swallows me up eagerly, her small breasts bouncing, her mouth open in wild pleasure. My cock doesn't even fit all the way inside her, and I marvel at the sight of it slipping in and out of her tiny, perfect cunt, the lips of her stretched wide to accommodate me.

It is truly a gift to be sunk in her, to clutch her bountiful ass in my hands and tug her closer to me, slinging her legs around my hips so I can take her even more thoroughly. She cries out with every one of my thrusts, and I don't care if her father hears us.

She is mine, all mine, and I will insist that she knows it every day for as long as she lives.

Soon, though, Simka grows annoyed at being underneath me and insists I lie on my back so she can guide us instead. In this position, I have to grit my teeth to keep from shooting off inside her as her channel clenches me gloriously, rippling and squeezing with every lift of her strong thighs.

"Are you going to take all of me?" I grunt, gripping her hips and shoving her down hard on my cock. Her moan is the most beautiful music. "All of my seed?"

"Every last drop," she says breathlessly, using me to reach her finish. I take over lifting her up by the hips as she rushes to the top of her peak, her eyes closing, her mouth falling open in a perfect circle. When she grips like iron around me, I can't help but follow her into our bottomless well of bliss.

She falls down on top of me, my cock still buried in her. Sweat dribbles off her brow as she sighs happily. I wrap my arms tight around her, kissing the top of her head, relishing how swollen her cunt is around me.

But I'm not finished yet. Seeing Gorren with a whelp of his own, I find I desperately want one for myself. I want to hold them close, to breathe in their smell, to watch my Simka curled up with them in her arms. So, I turn us onto our sides, and just at the thought of her full to bursting with me, I'm already stiffening up again.

Simka giggles. "Is that so?" She flexes her hips devilishly.

"Turn around," I tell her, and curiosity glistens in her eyes. She does as she's told, lying on the bed with her back facing me, dripping my seed between her legs. I slide my cock in once more, pushing all of it back into her.

Her heady moan is my reward. As I slowly take her, drawing out every single thrust, I wet my finger and drag it down between her two plush ass cheeks. I remember how she explored me with such curiosity—perhaps I'll give her a taste of how good it can be.

When I slip my finger inside her tiny, puckered hole, her moan is deep and surprised. I pump it in time with my cock, and soon she's crying out, telling everyone how good I feel inside her. When she's ready, I wiggle another finger into her ass, and her cunt tightens delightfully around me.

"H-h-how...?" she manages out, every part of her going rigid. "Oh, Jar'kel, I'm going to—"

Before she can finish her sentence, she's squeezing my cock so hard I have no choice but to burst. I jam myself deep, unleashing everything, imagining it all slipping in deep where it belongs. Until she is seeded, I will keep trying, giving her every pleasure imaginable.

Simka twitches as I remove my fingers. "Damn," she mutters as I press my palm to her abdomen, where I can feel myself inside her. "You're good at that."

I chuckle and kiss her head. "I couldn't do it without you."

CHAPTER 26

SIMKA

I thought it would be a bigger challenge to convince my village to accept Jar'kel as one of us. But word of the sacrifice he made for Vavi, though she's now left for the orc camp, spread quickly. He's treated as almost a curiosity, now that the threat of the wild orcs no longer hovers over us.

Though the neighbor makes it clear that she doesn't care for him much.

When the city guard came asking about "the troll prisoner," everyone pretended they had no idea. There's very little love for the city here among my people after they turned away our calls for help.

Though most of the soldiers had retreated once the orcs started blowing up rock and mine carts, many of the trollkin miners were trapped inside as the tunnels collapsed. My heart aches knowing so many lives were lost, but that was the cost of stopping the Grand Chieftain. Now he's chosen to withdraw, and Gorren has won.

If anything, having a big, rather terrifying-looking troll around gives the village some modicum of security. Should the trollkin return, he will protect us again and do what needs to be done.

After much grumping by my father about the noise Jar'kel and I make at night, we set to building our own house on the edge of town. Now, without all my time spent searching for Vavi, I'm able to find the game trail that brings the elk down in the summer, and finally carry home my own kill in a sledge that Fio pulls for me. The hunters at last let me into their circle, and while it will take me away from time to time, I can contribute how I've always wanted.

Jar'kel spends his days chopping wood and milling it, until the walls of our home are done enough that we can move out. Dad says he's grateful to be rid of us, but I think he's developed a soft spot for my troll, too. Though they are both grouches, Jar'kel is good at making himself useful, and I don't think my father can deny that I'm the happiest I've ever been.

Our house will be small but sturdy, with high ceilings so Jar'kel doesn't have to duck to get through the doorways. We build a great big bed, then add one adjoining room, with an unspoken agreement that we'll build more as we need them.

I know he still worries about the future, about a world where he isn't around any longer and what will become of me then. But that's a far-off speculation, I assure him. He doesn't let it stop us from trying our hardest to build the family that I know secretly, he's always wanted.

We're visiting the clan, high up on the mountain, when Vavi runs up to me to throw her arms around me in greeting. When she pulls away though, her mouth twists up and she tilts her head at me.

"You seem different," she says, her hands on her hips as she inspects me from head to toe. Her eyes dart over to Jar'kel. "Does she seem different to you?"

He looks baffled by the question. "She's still Simka," he says, then pinches my arm. "I think."

Gorren approaches us with Varn in his arms, who's wildly biting and clawing as he tries to escape his father's grip. The little boy has certainly recovered from his difficult entry into the world and has since become an utter hellion.

"Oh," the big orc says, a grin spreading across his face like he knows something we don't. "Silly troll." He elbows Jar'kel in the side. "The taste changes, you know."

Jar'kel blinks. "Is that what that is?" My mate wraps his arm around my middle and pulls me against him, bringing his mouth down to mine. "Are you full with me?"

I hadn't even thought about it. We've been so focused on our homesteading project that I'd forgotten we were trying.

"I suppose I haven't even noticed whether I've bled or not." I scratch my head.

Before I can blink, Jar'kel lifts me up off the ground and crushes me to his body, his tusks framing my cheeks. He kisses my mouth, my nose, my forehead, before nuzzling his face in my hair.

"That would be marvelous," he says in my ear, just for me, "if my beautiful woman is carrying my whelp."

I think what a good father he'll be, and kiss him back as hard as I can.

Vavi giggles. "I wonder what you'll get," she says, patting her own belly, which is swollen up with her second. "The other orc-human pairs here have had... mixed results."

"Mixed results?" Jar'kel asks.

"Some babies are orc, and some are human." She tilts her head. "We don't know why, but we have some theories."

Given what we've seen, there are likely even more unsolved mysteries in this world, each as wondrous as the last one.

JAR'KEL

By the time our home is finished and winter has covered the land in a deep layer of snow, my wild Simka has developed a rather pleasant bump under her fur coat. In the evenings we sit in front of the fire, her in my lap, my hands roaming from her swollen breasts to her rounded middle. Sometimes she takes me this way, too, riding me until her thighs give out and I turn her over onto her hands and knees. When the nights get long and the days short, sometimes we get adventurous, and I bury myself in her second entrance, exploring an entirely different pleasure. She likes to experiment on me, taking me in her mouth while she pumps one finger in and out of my own puckered hole, competing with herself to see how quickly she can make me shoot off.

Even as her belly gets bigger, and her breasts get ready to feed our whelp, my mate hungers for me. I would say she's insatiable, and my cock loves nothing more than to rise to the occasion and please her. I suck on her perfect nipples, and when I make her scream and clench down tight around me, lick up all the sweet milk that drizzles out.

She's everything I've ever wanted and didn't know it.

It may be a long, freezing winter, but I find I don't mind it at all. I never think of my desert, my position, or my corporal's coat. Now I wear furs from head to toe, soft leathers on my feet as they adjust to the cold, and I have more pairs of mittens than I know what to do with.

When it's finally time for our whelp to emerge, I feel more alive than I ever have. Whatever happens in the future, I have everything I need now. Simka's father and I have struck a truce, and we both wait with profound impatience.

But the moment comes when my mate should give birth, and

then it passes, and poor Simka only gets bigger and bigger. The midwife is worried, but none of us know much about human-trollkin pairings, so all we can do is wait and watch.

Vavi comes to visit with her two whelps, without Gorren, who would not be quite welcomed—not yet, anyway. The other humans who were taken once upon a time come and see their families, bringing their small children with them. In a way, they have united the clan and the village.

"You'll be fine," Vavi tells Simka as she lies on our bed. She often has to rest during the day, and it makes her quite annoyed that she can't go hunting. I promise her that as soon as our whelp is born, she and Fio can go and track all the elk she likes. Little Varn runs wild around the house while Vavi carries her new infant, who's as green and hefty as his father. One orc and one human— curious indeed.

"Magic knows what it's doing," Vavi says. "I promise."

"I just want this thing out of me," Simka grumbles. I kiss her hand, a little guilty my seed has led to so much discomfort. But she just grins at me. "It'll be worth it, though."

Simka is near bursting when finally, her big voice echoes all the way out in the woods, where I'm chopping down logs to keep the fire burning.

"*Jar'kel!*"

I won't pretend it isn't difficult to see my Simka in so much pain. She sobs miserably as Masha urges her to push harder, and then harder still. My mate clutches me tight and nearly strangles my hand with her sheer strength. But she is marvelous as she sweats her way through, though I'd never tell her that. Her determination is unmatched, and she roars like a bear as finally, the dam breaks, and she sags into the bed.

Masha's eyes are huge and round as she disconnects our whelp from her attachment to her mother. The small creature is blue, as blue as I am, with dark cobalt hair the same as mine. Her cry pierces the air, shrill and powerful, and I know then that while she might look like me, she's her mother's daughter through and through.

When at last the midwife has shown herself out and we're alone, I bring my Simka into my side, curling around her as our rather large whelp sucks at her nipple. After a few moments, though, our daughter stops again to wail, flinging her tiny hands in the air.

"How can she be crying when she has food right in front of her?" Simka grouches. She curls into me, too, so our screaming infant is wedged between us.

All I can do is laugh. "She's going to be a terror," I assure her. "And you have no one to blame but yourself."

We bicker about names for the rest of the night, until my mate and my whelp have fallen asleep in my arms. Then I lay my head down and let myself drift off next to them.

SIMKA

Jar'kel looks and acts younger than he ever has as our daughter grows up. He was right when he called her a terror. Kalli loves nothing more than to run into Fio's pen and throw her arms around his legs, and then one of us has to scramble in after her so my mule doesn't accidentally trample her. Fio just gives me a bored look, though, and eats his grain.

Dad visits every day, sometimes multiple times a day, just to see her. He found it odd at first, as did almost everyone else in the village, that she isn't remotely human. But now she plays with the other children like she's one of them. She's bigger, though, so sometimes Jar'kel has to pull her aside and remind her to watch her strength and size. When her tusks finally start to come in, she clings to him and cries her little heart out. He always holds her close, kissing the top of her head, until she feels better.

When my father takes Kalli away to play, and I've returned from the day's hunt, Jar'kel and I sneak inside the house and lock the door. It's much harder to get time to ourselves now, which I detest, and I tend to scream so loud I wake up the baby.

But Jar'kel has had a wicked look in his eye lately, and I want to find out what it's about.

The moment we're alone, I push him down to the floor in front of the fire and sit astride his hips. He lets out a surprisingly big laugh, and I love how every day, he gifts me with more and more laughs like that. His broken tusk pulls back with his smile, and I trace my fingers down his cheek to the laugh lines around his lips. That's what they are now.

My troll's eyelids drop low, and he tugs me in closer, keeping his arms clasped tight around my waist. He rubs his nose against mine.

"Simka," he whispers, for my ears only. He grinds our bodies together, and he's already at half-mast. Sometimes the older women in town joke about their husbands having a hard time getting it up, but my Jar'kel never flags in his duties. "I think our whelp needs a playmate, don't you? Someone who can keep up with her all day."

I inhale sharply as his thick lump rubs between my legs, telling me what it wants, and I want it just as much. He slides his hands up under my tunic, smoothing his palms over every plane of my body. I pin his hands against my breasts, and he eagerly plays with my nipples.

"That's what you want, is it?" I ask, pleasantly surprised. I wasn't sure he'd get the bug again after making one wild child together. "Another uncaged terror? Really?"

"Ah," he says with a groan. "I'll never stop wanting to see you big and round with my whelp." My handsome troll slides his hands over my hips, peeling down my leggings. "I wonder what other marvelous gifts we can create."

Once upon a time, I'd never have pegged him as sentimental. But now he wears his heart on his sleeve, polished and shining.

"Then we'd better get started," I say, shimmying off my pants before attacking his. Soon we're naked together on our bear rug, the flames reflecting off of Jar'kel's broad tusk. He starts readying me with his fingers, but I'm feeling hungry tonight, so I take his cock in my mouth and swallow him down as far as I can in one thrust. I love the way he comes apart between my lips, and his whole body shudders with his pleasure.

But his patience wears thin quickly. "On your knees," he tells me, and the sharpness in his voice cuts through any of my objections. When I'm sprawled in front of him, he licks me all over, thrusting his tongue inside me, tormenting me until I'm wriggling and desperate.

"Jar'kel," I whimper, rocking back against him, craving his return to where he belongs. He chuckles at my needy whines, but gives me exactly what I want.

It still tests my limits, taking him inside me. But oh, how he fills that space perfectly, as if our bodies were shaped for one another. He makes love to me steady and sure in front of the fire, until we both reach the end of our journey and jump off into the unknown together.

He runs his hand along my belly as we lie there, panting, his cock still full and swollen inside me. I reach down and squeeze the sac hanging below, and he moans as even more of his hot come shoots into me, dripping down my thigh.

"Simka," he chides. "That's how you milk a goat, not your mate's balls."

I bark a laugh, which makes me tighten up around him, and he jerks inside me. "I thought you wouldn't want to waste any."

When I glance over my shoulder, I find him wearing a wicked grin. We start all over again, me and my troll, our sweat mingling on each other's skin, imagining what our future holds.

Thank you for reading!

If you enjoyed this book, please consider leaving a review! Written reviews help authors like me reach new readers.

Join My Newsletter!

For all the latest regarding books, and to get a FREE Trollkin Lovers novella, join my newsletter! You can also find signed paperbacks and artwork of your favorite books.

www.LyonneRiley.com

ALSO BY LYONNE RILEY

TROLLKIN LOVERS

Stealing the Troll's Heart

Healing the Orc's Heart

Capturing the Orc's Heart

Charming the Troll's Heart

Keeping the Human's Heart

Tempting the Ogre's Heart

Enchanting the Ogre's Heart

ANTHOLOGIES

The Monster Menagerie

STANDALONES

Prince of Beasts

My Minotaur Husband

ABOUT THE AUTHOR

I come from a traditional publishing background, which is rewarding but often too rigid, so I shifted to self-publishing to pursue my real passion in writing: extremely sexy non-human romance. I probably should have known I would end up here after spending most of my young adulthood writing erotic fan fiction, but it took me a while to find my way back to myself.

Acknowledgments

I would like to thank everyone involved in helping me through the process of putting out this book. I can't say enough how much I appreciate the help and encouragement of the people around me—especially Amber, who told me I could do this in the first place.

Huge thank you to Rowan Woodcock for the gorgeous cover illustration. To my critique partners, who gave me phenomenal feedback: You all make this possible. And of course, my amazing spouse, who has always supported my dreams—and given me lots of inspiration for my characters' sexy adventures.

I couldn't have done this without the expertise of my fellow self-published romance authors. Thank you for inviting me into your circles and helping me through this process.

And thank you to my readers, who gave this book a shot.